BEHIND THE WHITE VEIL

The CHERRY AMES *Stories*

☆　　☆　　☆

The VICKI BARR *Flight Stewardess Series*

"So you found it——" said again."

Behind the Wind-Veil

"So *you* found them," he said again.

Behind the White Veil

BEHIND THE WHITE VEIL

BY JULIE TATHAM

GROSSET & DUNLAP

PUBLISHERS

New York

CONTENTS

BEHIND THE WHITE VEIL

CHAPTER I

An Invitation

THE HUGE SILVER PLANE SOARED ABOVE SEATTLE'S lakes and lofty hills. As it climbed high into the sky Vicki unbuckled her safety belt. She had had her vacation, a week in glamorous Hawaii, and now she was glad to be back in the trim blue uniform of a Federal Airlines stewardess.

Vicki loved her job and knew that she would enjoy every minute of the Seattle-to-Juneau, Alaska, run. There was only one thing wrong; Victoria Barr was homesick. Ever since she had become a flight stewardess she had only had time for flying visits home. It seemed to her that she would be just settling down for a long, heart-to-heart talk with her pretty, young-thinking mother when a telegram would arrive, sending her off to another assignment. Vicki loved to travel, especially by air, but the present run, due to an emergency, had rushed her straight from San Francisco to Federal's office in

1

Seattle. She had counted on being flown back to headquarters in New York via Chicago with an overnight stopover there so that she could visit her family in near-by Fairview. And she had looked forward to telling her parents and her twelve-year-old sister, Ginny, about her exciting experiences in the Hawaiian Islands.

"Well," she decided, smoothing her silvery blond bob, "there's no sense in moping. I've got work to do."

First she must see if all her passengers were comfortable, and then it would be time to prepare and serve lunch. She consulted her manifest for clues to the personalities of her various guests. Vicki always felt like a hostess when she was on duty. The comfortable, up-to-date ship was her air-borne apartment, and the little galley in the back, her kitchenette. Ruth Benson, Federal's assistant superintendent of flight stewardesses, had written Vicki that most of the passengers probably would be business men, "regular commuters between 'The Gateway to the North' and Alaska's capital.

"But it won't be dull," Ruth had continued, "for you're bound to have at least one fascinating character on every flight. There'll be one or two old-time Yukoners, now on the trail of uranium, copper, silver, tin, lead, or platinum deposits. They used to travel by dog sled or shanks' mare (their own legs), but a few are now prospecting from the air. You'll probably meet men who can tell you how they made

a fortune in the salmon and seal industries. You won't have any Eskimo passengers for they hunt and fish too far north. But you may have to cope with an Indian family on a holiday, and then you'll need all the tact and patience in the world. For Indian children, like Eskimo children, do not know the meaning of the word discipline. They are allowed to eat, sleep, cry, and play whenever it suits their fancy."

And, sure enough, on her very first flight that morning, Vicki had ushered aboard an Indian father and mother with three round-faced, beady-eyed youngsters. Remembering Ruth's warning, she glanced apprehensively down the aisle toward their seats. Then her blue eyes popped open with horror.

The eldest boy was busily engaged in hacking himself free of his seat belt with the largest and sharpest hunting knife Vicki had ever seen. Placidly, even proudly, his parents watched. In a split second Vicki was out of her seat and halfway down the aisle. But before she could reach the boy, a strapping, red-haired woman already had intervened.

In the back of her mind Vicki realized that this plump but brisk lady passenger was the wife of George Hyacith, professor of archaeology at the University of Washington, who was dozing in his seat.

"Here, you," Mrs. Hyacith was shouting as her large hand shot deftly across the aisle to grab the boy's brown wrist. "Drop it, or I'll turn you across my knee and paddle the daylights out of you."

"Sakey do no harm," the father growled while the mother's heavy black brows drew together in a threatening scowl. Vicki wouldn't have been at all surprised if more knives appeared.

"Tact and patience," she thought with an inward sniff. "They should have provided me with a coat of armor."

Breathlessly she skidded to a stop by the boy's seat and smiled her thanks to Mrs. Hyacith.

"Of course Sakey didn't mean any harm," she told the glowering parents. "These buckles *are* hard to unfasten." Somehow she forced herself to ignore the little brown hand holding the dangerous knife, and bent down to loosen the belt.

The minute the child was free good humor was restored to the whole family.

"Sakey smart," the mother said as fatuously as though Vicki were in full agreement.

"Smart!" This was a hiss from Mrs. Hyacith whose round, freckled face was still red with anger. "You'd better let me take that weapon away from him, stewardess, and wallop him with my magazine!"

Vicki laughed nervously. "I was just going to suggest, Sakey," she said, "that you might like to cut out some pictures in those magazines in the rack by your mother's seat. If you'll let me borrow your knife to cut up the meat for your little sister's lunch, I'll lend you my scissors."

Instantly the boy surrendered the knife. With the superior air of one who had lived a couple of years

longer than the other two children, he said, "Muska is very clumsy. She can't cut anything without cutting her fingers. You can cut up her meat, but I can cut up my own."

"Of course you can," Vicki said soothingly, hoping that by the time lunch was served he would be willing to use one of the airlines' gleaming silver knives instead of his own razor-edged blade.

"He should be spanked and made to take his nap without lunch," Mrs. Hyacith muttered, and then added in a whisper to Vicki:

"Don't mind me. My bark's worse than my bite. If you're worried for fear those imps will wreck the interior of the plane while you're fixing lunch, don't. I'll tell them stories to keep them out of mischief. Way back, when we were first out of college, my husband and I were Indian Service teachers, at a Yukon school. The kids' parents were the bane of our existence, but the children themselves behaved beautifully in the classroom. They love to study, think of it as a game. I'll amuse them by taking them on a mental tour through the university's museum."

"Wonderful," replied Vicki gratefully.

Mrs. Hyacith's frail-looking husband woke up then and said to no one in particular, "Miss Barr handled that contretemps with tact and expeditiousness."

Vicki's fair skin flamed with color. So he hadn't been dozing!

He stared up at her name in the placard at the

front of the plane and said reminiscently, "Barr. Um-m. I went to college with a very handsome, blond young gentleman named Lewis Marvell Barr. He was at that time aspiring to be an instructor in economics, but it was the consensus of opinion that he would end up a chef. My, what he couldn't do with cheese, eggs, and a chafing dish!"

"He hasn't changed a bit, Dr. Hyacith," Vicki said with a giggle. "Lewis Marvell Barr is my father. During the week he's professor of economics at State University, but on Sundays he dons his chef's cap and invades our kitchen. And he's just as tall, blond, and handsome as he was when you knew him."

"Indeed?" Professor Hyacith smiled warmly. "I might have guessed that you were Lewis' daughter, for you have inherited his good looks and blond coloring, although you are as small as he is tall. After you have performed your duties you must come and sit with us while I plague you with questions. Your father was a freshman when I was a senior. I lost sight of him after I was graduated. Now, if you will, I'd like to be brought up to date."

"I'd be delighted," Vicki assured him. The tiny lump of homesickness swelled in her throat as she hurried back to her galley. Still, she wouldn't change jobs with anyone else in the world. For her various assignments since graduation, which had taken her up and down the East Coast, to Memphis, New Orleans, Mexico, and Central America, had each one been an exciting adventure.

If only after her vacation in Honolulu she could have flown home for an hour or two. But there had been just time for a frantic wire asking her mother to pack her uniforms and send them on the first Federal plane out of Chicago to the Seattle hotel. They had arrived shortly after Vicki herself had reported for duty at the Seattle headquarters.

There she had been delighted to find waiting for her a long letter from Ruth Benson. The handsome young assistant flight superintendent had once been on the Seattle-to-Juneau run herself and was able to pass along to Vicki several valuable hints.

"It's too bad," she had written in closing, "that we had to rush you from the tropics to the frozen north, but the gal who had the job before you suddenly up and eloped. Don't you dare fall in love with some daring young bush pilot and follow suit! As you probably know, the bush pilots are Alaska's air-borne sourdoughs, which means pioneers. The word comes from the batter which the early miners always kept in crocks for their pancakes, bread, and biscuits. As often as not, that's all they had to eat, and in freezing weather they would take their crocks to bed with them to keep the batter from freezing."

Thinking of sourdough reminded Vicki of Mrs. Duff's delicious popovers. Mrs. Duff was the plump, jolly woman who kept house for Vicki and five other flight stewardesses who shared an apartment with her in New York. And thinking of *them* reminded her that she hadn't yet had time even to drop them

all postcards telling them of her new assignment.

"I'll send Mrs. Duff a wire when we land in Juneau," Vicki decided as she popped the lunches into the oven. "And before the return flight I'll buy them all little souvenirs of Alaska."

She could hardly wait to go sight-seeing in Alaska's capital, which she knew nestled at the foot of the Juneau and Roberts mountains. Ruth Benson had written that from the air it looked as though these thirty-six-hundred-feet-high mountains were trying to force the city into the channel.

"And except for the brief summer months," she had warned Vicki, "it rains or snows almost all the time. But just as the Hawaiians pay no attention to their 'liquid sunshine,' Juneau citizens don't let the precipitation bother them, either."

Vicki shivered now in anticipation. A fragrant mist falling from tropical mountains was one thing; a December rain in the far north, quite another. And she was grateful that her mother had sent along with the uniforms a practical but attractive present from the whole family.

Vicki had crowed with delight when she unpacked the box and saw the scarlet waterproof coat and hood with its warm detachable fleece lining. Pinned to a pocket was a scribbled note from Vicki's sister Ginny:

"I earned the money for my share of this myself, Little Red Riding Hood. While you were basking on the beach at Waikiki, Cookie and I were slaving

week ends and after school. Working as delivery girls in Fairview, I'll have you know. I've dragged sledfuls of groceries at least a million miles, but the tips I got were worth it. The only sad part about it is that I didn't lose a pound! Everybody met me at the kitchen door with hot chocolate, thick with whipped cream, and slabs of the most fattening kind of cake and cookies. I didn't want to hurt their feeling by refusing.

"Oh, Vic," she had finished mournfully, "will I ever get as slim as you? I don't have to wear my glasses any more or those hideous shoes, but I can't seem to stick to a reducing diet."

Vicki had written a hasty thank-you-and-much-love" letter to her parents, adding a P.S. to Ginny:

"Don't worry, Sis. Some day you'll find yourself as slim as a cricket without even trying. And a million thanks for your share of the darling red coat you all sent me."

An hour later luncheon was over. Sakey and his brother and sister were napping across the aisle, having eaten with record speed everything on the trays Vicki brought them. There had been no mention of the knife which Vicki had left in the galley.

"I'm terrified for fear he'll wake up and demand it any minute," she told Mrs. Hyacith.

"Now, don't you go and borrow trouble," the plump woman scolded. "He may sleep right through until we land. I'll bet none of them even closed their eyes last night. In summer when there is almost no

night a whole family may stay awake for three days at a time. Nobody ever thinks of telling an Eskimo or Indian child to go to bed."

"My sister would love that kind of a nonschedule," Vicki said with a laugh. "Ever since I can remember she's been inventing excuses to stay up later than she is allowed. The last one was that she got seasick if she was forced to retire before she was practically asleep on her feet."

Professor Hyacith chuckled. "It is hard for me to be convinced that Lewis Barr is a stern parent."

"Oh, he isn't," Vicki assured him. "They're both the most wonderfully understanding parents in the world. Dad wanted terribly for me to continue on at college, but when he realized that I had set my heart on becoming a flight stewardess, he gave in without a murmur. And as for Mother, if she'd been within the age limit she would probably have filed an application blank with Federal before I did. Not that she really would ever leave Dad and Ginny alone in The Castle. Between his intricate menus and Ginny's fudge they'd probably burn the house down to the ground."

She told the Hyaciths then about the Barr home on the crest of a hill at the edge of Fairview.

"We call it The Castle," she said, "although it's not really very big, but it has a tower and high Norman casement windows and an upstairs balcony."

She stopped suddenly because the tiny lump in her throat had grown to the size of a golf ball.

"You sound like a rather homesick young stewardess." Mrs. Hyacith's usually crisp voice was soft with sympathy.

Vicki determinedly swallowed the golf ball. "I am," she admitted with a gulp. "Oh, I love traveling all over the United States and flying to foreign countries, but if only just once I'd get a short assignment near home!"

Mrs. Hyacith stared at her in amazement. "Why waste your energies wishing?" she demanded. "All you have to do is let that nice Miss Benson you were telling us about know how you feel. I'm sure she can arrange it. This is just a temporary assignment, isn't it?"

Vicki nodded.

"Well, then," Mrs. Hyacith went on briskly, "if I were you I'd get off a letter to my boss as soon as possible. It seems to me you've been up in the air a lot ever since you got out of school. Maybe without knowing it you're due to be grounded soon. In that case why not request duty in Chicago? It's not far from Fairview, is it?"

"I never thought of that," Vicki said, cheering up immediately. "Ruth Benson did ask me just before I went on my vacation if I'd consider training for a job similar to hers. I said, no thank you, ma'am, because I thought that would mean being grounded in New York, too far away from The Castle. But she might have been thinking of a job nearer home." She clasped her knees ecstatically. "I'll write her a letter

from the Juneau airport and tell her I'm suffering from a spot of homesickness. She's almost as understanding a person as my curly-haired mother, so if it can be wangled, she'll wangle it."

"That's right," Mrs. Hyacith said approvingly. "And in the meantime, Hy and I want you to have dinner with us your first free night in Seattle. We're flying back home ourselves tomorrow right after Hy's lecture."

"If," her husband put in quietly, "all of our business can be concluded by then, Jenny."

"Oh, it will be," Mrs. Hyacith said airily. "Max is a very competent bush pilot. We can leave all the details to him. After all, Hy, with the prompt answers you got to your ad, there's no reason for delaying the exploratory flight any longer than it'll take Max to tell us how much it will cost. And no matter what it costs, you know perfectly well you'll never be happy until you've located that hot springs valley. I may have to beg, borrow, or steal the money, but—"

She stopped suddenly and her plump face turned so red that for a moment the numerous freckles were completely obliterated. Vicki, sensing that Mrs. Hyacith had said more than she meant to in front of a stranger, jumped to her feet.

"It's awfully kind of you to ask homesick me to dinner," she said hastily, hoping they would think she hadn't heard. "Do you really want me?"

"Of course we do, my dear," Professor Hyacith

told her warmly, while his wife sat silently biting her full, red lips. "Jenny will write down our phone number for you. I never can remember it myself." His thin, stooped shoulders shook with silent laughter. "I am the absent-minded professor to end all absent-minded professors. Would you believe it? When I received the first reply to the 'share-the-flight' advertisement I inserted in the Seattle morning paper I was momentarily confused. I suppose I can be excused because, although I wrote the notice myself, it was really at Jenny's suggestion. And since the letter was concerned mainly with the gentleman's desire to ascertain whether or not uranium—"

His wife found her voice then. "HY!" she exploded, and quickly said to Vicki, "We mustn't bore you with our private worries, Miss Barr. When will you have a free night in Seattle?"

Vicki, feeling confused and uncomfortable, stammered out a weak, "Thursday night. But if that's inconvenient—"

"Inconvenient?" Professor Hyacith's sandy eyebrows shot up in surprise. "My dear, I was just thinking that we have a not too uncomfortable day bed in my study. There is no reason why Lewis Barr's daughter should stay on at a hotel, especially since I shall be away from home for at least a week once we have discovered the actual existence of what, I must confess, seems to me almost too good to be true. Imagine such a phenomenon in the Alaska Range—"

"You're quite right, Hy," his wife interrupted

soothingly. "Miss Barr could keep me company while you're away gathering material for another lecture." She wrote down their address and telephone number on a card she snatched out of her huge, overflowing handbag, talking all the while. "But first Miss Barr must see our little apartment and decide whether that day bed is too uncomfortable or not." She handed the card to Vicki. "Then it's all settled. Thursday evening at seven."

"You're very kind," Vicki said with a grateful smile. And then to her surprise the NO SMOKING —FASTEN YOUR SEAT BELT sign flashed on up in front. Time had passed so quickly that she had had no idea they were approaching the airport ten miles from the heart of Juneau.

The three Indian children slept peacefully as she helped their parents strap them in. When Vicki promised to return the razor-edged knife to Sakey before he left the plane, his father shook his head with a broad grin.

"You keep," he said. "Many more like that at home. You need more than Sakey. Knives you have no good for cutting up meat."

There was no time to protest and Vicki decided to accept the present as a souvenir of her first flight to Alaska rather than to risk hurting the Indian's feelings.

Back in her own seat, Vicki stared down at Gastineau Channel, a narrow strip of green water, a dark strip against the mountains, deep in snow. It

was one of those rare clear afternoons, and she caught a glimpse of the ski slope on Douglas across the channel and of what she guessed must be one of the seven glaciers which flow from the Coast Range icecap.

But she was not thinking of the sight-seeing she would do in Juneau before the return flight the next morning. She couldn't help wondering about the "share-the-flight" ad Professor Hyacith had put in the Seattle morning paper, to which he had apparently received a reply from a prospector interested in uranium. And there were other provocative phrases in the conversation which kept coming back in her mind, although she tried to dismiss them as none of her business. A very competent young bush pilot . . . exploratory flight . . . a hot springs valley . . . a phenomenon in the Alaska Range . . .

None of it made much sense to Vicki, but her curiosity was aroused just the same. Especially since Mrs. Hyacith had obviously regretted letting Vicki hear as much as she had.

As the plane circled for a landing Vicki tried to dismiss the matter from her mind. But she couldn't help wondering how there could be a warm springs valley in the midst of the everlasting snows of the Alaska Range.

CHAPTER II

The Share-the-Flight Plan

THURSDAY EVENING ON THE DOT OF SEVEN VICKI knocked on the door of the Hyaciths' ground-floor apartment in Seattle's residential section. They had flown back with her Tuesday morning on the return flight from Juneau, and again warmly repeated their invitation. Vicki also guessed from their high spirits that their business there had been satisfactorily concluded.

But no more mention—at least not in front of her —had been made of a hot springs valley in the Alaska Range. Vicki was now beginning to think that the existence of such a valley was a figment of eccentric Professor Hyacith's imagination. The Federal pilots she had talked with since Monday had crisscrossed the Alaska Range dozens of times.

"If there's a warm valley anywhere among those ice-capped mountains I would have seen it," one of them had told Vicki emphatically. "Somebody's been trying to take you for a ride."

"Not that it matters," Vicki reflected now, speaking out loud without realizing it.

"What doesn't matter?" a voice behind her demanded.

She whirled embarrassedly around to look up into the tanned face of a tall young man with a thick crop of black, curly hair. "Doesn't it matter whether anyone answers your knock or not?" he asked, his dark eyes twinkling. "Me, I'm hungry."

Vicki laughed. "Me too. The people who live behind this door invited me to dinner, but I guess they forgot all about it. Professor Hyacith is admittedly absent-minded, but I didn't think his wife was."

"She is anything but," the young man assured her. "They invited me to dinner too, and I guess Jenny is way back in the kitchen fixing it. So let's knock more loudly and then introduce ourselves." He hammered on the heavy panel with a big brown fist and said, "I'm Max Lowler, ex-flying agent for the Fish and Wildlife Service. Now an independent pilot with a fast six-passenger Bellanca which will be my own after one more payment."

"Oh," Vicki gasped. "Then you must be the bush pilot—"

At that moment the door opened and Mrs. Hyacith stood on the threshold, beaming at them both. "I see you two young people have introduced yourselves. Come in, come in, and don't forget to admire the red velvet smoking jacket Hy is wearing in honor of the occasion. We don't often have the privilege of

entertaining a pilot and a flight stewardess at dinner."

She bustled ahead of them into the living room without giving them a chance to say good evening. The young pilot whispered to Vicki as they followed their hostess,

"A flight stewardess, huh?"

Vicki nodded. "I'm Vicki Barr of Federal Airlines. On the Seattle-to-Juneau run."

"Then that," he said, "makes us first cousins. My headquarters is Juneau. I was born in Seattle, but spent most of my life in Alaska. So we can dispense with formalities and start right out on a first-name basis. Okay, Vic?"

"Okay, Max," she said, and then crossed the room to shake hands with her host who did, indeed, look very distinguished in his handsome jacket. "It matches my new coat," she said, pushing back the hood and unfastening the zipper.

It was now Professor Hyacith's turn to admire Vicki. "It's very becoming," he said, "and as practical as an Eskimo parka. You know, the Eskimos are able to endure extreme cold not, as is commonly believed, because they have become hardened to it. The truth of the matter is that they dress sensibly. First, an Eskimo dons a suit with the fur side inside, then over that he wears one with the fur side outside, both with hoods. If it is snowing he wears a cotton shirt over both suits. Then, with fur mittens and sealskin boots, he stays as warm as though he

were in a thermos bottle, although the temperature may be sixty below zero."

"But what about his face?" Vicki asked. "I should think his nose would turn to ice in a few minutes. Mine always feels as though it were frostbitten in cold weather."

"It's easy enough to avoid frostbite," Mrs. Hyacith said as she passed fragile cups of steaming bouillon. "As soon as you feel a spot on your face is freezing, you slip your arm out of the sleeve of your coat and push it up through the neck of your parka. Then you press it on the cold spot and your own body warmth thaws you out."

"It's what happens to the babies that fascinates me," Max said, settling down on the sofa between his hostess and Vicki. Professor Hyacith sat opposite them, dreamily sucking on his pipe.

"What does happen to Eskimo babies?" Vicki asked.

"Their mothers carry them pickaback fashion inside their coats," Max said. "And often on a long journey the infant gets too hot inside that thermos, so he cries in protest. Then the mother spreads a skin on the snow and places the naked child on it, no matter how many degrees below zero it may be. The baby plays happily until it shows signs that it's had enough cold, then it's slipped back inside the mother's coat. Why they don't catch pneumonia is beyond me."

"It makes me shiver to think about it," Vicki said.

She turned to her hostess. "I love your apartment. It's so warm and cheerful and comfortable. The minute I stepped inside this room I forgot that it's winter."

Mrs. Hyacith's broad face beamed with pleasure. "I'm a great lover of all creature comforts," she said. "I don't know a thing about interior decorating, but I think a living room ought to have a lived-in look. The only trouble with our furniture is that once I get comfortably settled down on a chair or a sofa, it takes a derrick to get me out." She heaved herself to her feet, panting and chuckling. "Come and see the other rooms, Vicki, and then we'll have dinner. The two men have business to discuss."

The rest of the apartment, Vicki discovered, was as cheerful as the living room, and the day bed in the professor's study looked invitingly comfortable.

"It's all settled, Hy," Mrs. Hyacith called from the doorway of the den. "Vicki accepts our invitation. Now that she has promised to keep me company I won't mind so much when you go off on that reconnaissance fli—"

Suddenly she stopped. "Oh, it's all so silly, Hy," she exploded. "Why should we keep our little secret from Vicki? One would think we were going to do something criminal!"

"I agree with you, Jenny," he said. "But the other passengers requested—"

"I don't care what they requested," she cried impatiently. "What difference does it make if the

whole world and Vicki Barr in particular knows about our expedition?"

"None, so far as I am concerned," he said in his quiet voice. "And since we were not sworn to secrecy I am in favor of telling Vicki the whole story."

"Then we'll do it over dinner," his wife said. "If that duck stays in the oven another minute it'll quack."

"Or cry like an overheated Eskimo baby," Vicki said with a laugh as they all trooped into the cozy, informal dining room. "Yummy-yum. Something smells delicious."

"If I do say so myself," Mrs. Hyacith said as her husband began to carve, "my mashed potato stuffing is the best in the world. I use sage and onion, salt and pepper, and lots of butter. Do you think your father would like the recipe, Vicki?"

"I'm sure he would," Vicki said. And when she had tasted the hot chestnut sauce that was served with the duck, she asked for that recipe too.

"Remember to tell him that it's no good unless he uses a pint of heavy cream," Mrs. Hyacith said, passing a huge bowl of wild rice to Vicki. "My goodness, it's no wonder I'm fat."

The professor, Vicki couldn't help noticing, ate almost nothing while his wife heaped her own plate high and consumed every morsel with evident relish. After nibbling at a piece of meat and toying with a lettuce leaf, he laid down his fork.

"I'm sure, my dear," he said to Vicki, "that you've

been wondering about the expedition we referred to a while ago."

Vicki's mouth was so full she could only nod in reply.

"To begin at the beginning," he said, "we must go back to last summer. Jenny and I spent part of our holiday at Mt. McKinley Park. Mt. McKinley, as you undoubtedly know, is approximately four miles high and is the highest peak in North America. While I was perusing the newspaper one evening I was attracted to a small item on one of the back pages. It stated undramatically, and obviously with tongue in cheek, that a prospector was spreading a fantastic tale all along the west bank of the Susitna River. This prospector claimed to have discovered a fabulous valley in the Alaska Range the winter before. He insisted that while flying over the mountains in his helicopter, he caught a glimpse of green trees and an unfrozen stream lined with grassy banks. Naturally he hovered in mid-air, staring down in astonishment, and then a veil of fog cut off his view. No one paid any attention to him, but at last the story reached the ears of a newspaper reporter who wrote it up, stating that obviously the gentleman had seen a snow mirage. But I began to wonder."

Mrs. Hyacith stopped eating long enough to tell Vicki, "You see, we once knew a trapper who told us he had spent a winter in a 'steam-heated' valley within seven degrees of the Arctic Circle. And we'd

also heard of an expedition organized by a group of natural scientists who claimed to have located a semitropical valley near the British-Columbia–Yukon boundary."

"I've heard over and over again of valleys fed by hot springs," Max added. "An old miner told me about one where he said there were enormous ferns and tangled vines of berries the size of peaches, in winter, mind you. You know, of course, Vicki, that all Alaskan crops during the long summer days grow to jumbo size. You should see the flowers that grow around Juneau during our brief summer!"

"I'd like to," Vicki said. "I've seen pictures of blue meadows of lupine, and fields flaming with marigolds. But I can't believe anything grows in the Alaska Range during the winter."

"It is a tantalizing reflection," Professor Hyacith said dreamily. "So tantalizing that after reading that newspaper account, I obtained the prospector's name and address from the editor. I wrote at once and finally received a reply, arranging an interview at his rooming house in Anchorage. Once I had seen the man and received more details, I was convinced of the authenticity of his tale."

He lightly sketched a little map on the tablecloth. "From Mr. Smith's description, I am ready to believe that fauna and flora could flourish in such a hot springs valley until subzero temperatures from above finally counteracted the effect of the springs. The floor is only about eight miles long and less

than a mile across at its widest point. Halfway up the east wall a broad shelf juts, and looming protectively from the north is a tall, snow-clad mountain peak. Thus the floor is sheltered from the bitter northeast wind, and the snow must turn to rain when it comes in contact with the warm air near the surface of the ground."

"I see," Vicki said, thoughtfully staring at the crude map. "The shelf and the cliff act as umbrellas, shielding two-thirds of the valley. And the dense forests you've shown in the unprotected areas are the result of almost constant precipitation."

"Exactly." The professor beamed at her. "The point that convinced me of the authenticity of Mr. Smith's story, is that the valley is protected on the north and east. One of the reasons why our own fair city has mild temperatures the year round is that we are shielded by the Cascade Mountains. Why, my dear, here in Seattle one can play golf almost every day of the year."

"Stop him," Jenny boomed, grinning broadly. "Don't let him get started on the subject of our marvelous climate."

"Then what happened?" Vicki asked the professor tactfully. "Did you come straight back home after you saw Mr. Smith?"

"I did," he told her, "and endeavored to interest the trustees of the university in financing at least a reconnaissance expedition by air. But to no avail," he said sadly. "Last month I received the verdict

that even if such a valley did exist, it would take too much time and money to locate it."

His wife interrupted with a sniff. "One of the trustees, a good friend of ours, implied that if Hy wanted to go exploring by balloon, he thought it was a wonderful idea, but the money for such an expedition would have to come out of his own pocket." She dropped her knife and fork with an angry clatter. "I knew my husband would die of a broken heart if he didn't at least try to find that valley, so I put on my thinking cap, which I rarely do because it makes my head ache to think about anything more momentous than how much cinnamon I should put in the applesauce."

"That is a gross misrepresentation of the truth," Professor Hyacith corrected her with a fond smile. "Jenny is the genius of this family. When she laid on my desk that share-the-ride advertisement she clipped out of the paper and asked me if it gave me an idea, I admitted quite truthfully that it didn't."

"Oh, come now, Hy," she scolded. "I was so proud of having any idea at all, I didn't give you a chance to think. I just blurted out that if people could advertise for passengers to share the expenses of trips by automobile, why couldn't we insert a 'share-the-flight' ad? Then Hy promptly wrote up such a very clever notice that we received three replies the next day."

"I must say," her husband continued, "that I had not anticipated such immediate and enthusiastic re-

actions. Why, young Mr. Brossard must have telephoned us before the ink was dry on the newspaper."

"And that sourdough wasn't far behind him," Mrs. Hyacith said. "Such a fascinating old man, Vicki. A Mr. Mordecaw, one of the original Yukoners. I could sit and listen to him talk forever, couldn't you, Hy?"

"Oh, yes, indeed," the professor agreed. "And the young engineer is a most interesting person too, in my opinion. Mr. Chapman's firm," he told Vicki, "is sending him along on the expedition in order to ascertain the possibilities of a hydraulic engineering project in the valley. If there is one."

"And Mr. Mordecaw is looking for gold, I imagine," Vicki said.

"No, uranium," Mrs. Hyacith corrected her. "Like the prospector Hy interviewed in Anchorage, Mr. Mordecaw says he also caught a glimpse of the valley from his helicopter. Only the fog veil didn't fall until he'd had more than a glimpse. Mr. Mordecaw noticed the rock formation and feels that there may be uranium ore under the rim of the shelf."

"Oh," Vicki said thoughtfully. "Now that you've met another witness you can be pretty sure that there is such a valley?"

"That's right," Mrs. Hyacith said. "Mr. Mordecaw's valley is in almost the exact location where the Anchorage prospector said his was."

"But why didn't Mr. Mordecaw land there himself

in his helicopter?" Vicki asked. "I shouldn't think he would have wasted any time establishing his claim. Uranium ore is the raw material of atomic energy, isn't it? And didn't I read somewhere that the government pays a ten-thousand-dollar reward for the discovery of a high-grade deposit of at least twenty tons?"

"That's absolutely true," Max said with a sigh of satisfaction now that he had eaten every scrap on his plate. "I can't imagine why that old sourdough wants to share the flight with you, Professor Hyacith. You'd think that the last thing he'd want to do would be to share the secret of his discovery until after he has filed a formal claim."

"I can explain that," the professor said calmly. "Mr. Mordecaw was almost out of fuel when he hovered above the valley. Furthermore, he was almost out of funds, and the helicopter was a rented one." He cleared his throat suggestively. "I have looked into the financial end of renting helicopters and I assure you it is a most expensive proposition. In comparison, contributing one-fourth of what Max is going to charge for his services, is a mere bagatelle."

"And as for the sharing-the-secret angle," Mrs. Hyacith added, "Mr. Mordecaw begged us, practically on his bended knees, to keep the whole expedition under our hats. Those were his very words," she finished with a laugh. "And now for dessert. If you'll clear the table, Vicki, I'll slice the

lightest angel cake that was ever baked. It should be good; the whites of eleven eggs went into it."

"Oh me, oh my," Max groaned as he helped Vicki carry plates through the swinging door to the kitchen sink. "I never would have had that third helping of duck smothered in chestnut sauce if I'd known cake was in the offing."

"Don't talk behind your hostess's back," Mrs. Hyacith informed him tartly. "My cake is nothing but froth. And if a man of your height, with shoulders as broad as yours are, can't eat as much as I can, things have come to a pretty pass."

"Don't judge people's appetites by their circumferences," Max said, grinning. "Pint-size Vicki ate almost as much as I did and she's watering at the mouth for dessert."

"It's a fib," Vicki said, deliberately widening her eyes and licking her lips as Mrs. Hyacith cut the cake into huge slices. Then she sobered. "What about the third passenger, Mrs. Hyacith? The young Mr. Brossard? Why is he joining the expedition?"

"A budding author," she told Vicki. "He has already set up a group of conflicting characters whom he wants to place in some isolated and almost inaccessible spot where they can conflict with each other for a hundred thousand words."

"But surely," Vicki said, "there is no reason for secrecy in his case. I can understand Mr. Chapman's firm wishing to avoid possible competition from another engineering outfit, but I should think

a writer would welcome publicity about the background of his proposed novel. The more it gets, the better his book will sell."

"Not necessarily," Mrs. Hyacith said as she stacked the cake plates on a large tray. "Suppose a well-known novelist hears about that valley and uses it as the background for a book of his own? Young Mr. Brossard wouldn't have a chance then of interesting a publisher. And he's such a nice, earnest young man, Vicki. I'm sure if you knew him you'd keep our secret for his sake alone."

"I won't tell a soul," Vicki promised. Back in the dining room, she said to Max, "But before you take off from the Anchorage airport you'll have to file a flight plan, won't you?"

"Sure," he said easily. "But I'll simply say I'm piloting a private sight-seeing tour of that vicinity. Which is all the reconnaissance flight will be anyway."

Vicki frowned. "But will that sound logical to an airline official? I shouldn't think anybody would want to fly over those ice-capped mountain peaks in winter unless he had to."

"It'll sound perfectly logical to an Alaskan," he assured her. "They're the world's most air-minded people. Expensive though flying is, traveling by dog sled is much more expensive. And in a country where there are so few roads, sight-seeing on horseback or by car is hopeless. Actually, I'd rather fly in Alaska in midwinter than in summer, due to cli-

matic conditions, and also I'd rather fly in Alaska than anywhere else in the world."

"That just doesn't make sense," Vicki argued.

"Yes, it does," he insisted. "In central Alaska during the winter fogs are rare and the skies are usually clear. The reason why there's a veil over that valley most of the time must be obvious to you, a flight stewardess."

Vicki nodded understandingly. "That mist is caused by the hot air below meeting the cold air above. It must be like the fog that drapes the whole eastern seaboard when a hot front and cold front meet."

"To put it more simply," Mrs. Hyacith said with her loud, hearty laugh, "it's the same old steam that forms on the windowpane of a heated room in winter. And the moisture that drips off the outside of a glass of ice water in summer."

"Very well put," Professor Hyacith said approvingly. "My theory is that we will run into less precipitation during this first week in December than we would have earlier when the wooded area below the mountain peaks would have retained so much radiant heat from the sun. In the spring, summer, and fall, the valley is undoubtedly blanketed in mist or rain most of the time, which would explain the lush growth on the floor." He rubbed his thin hands together excitedly. "At this time of the year the temperature below should be equalizing itself with the temperature above, for of course the hot springs

could not hope to battle the bitter cold indefinitely." He stood up without having touched a fork to his dessert. "The meteorological forecast for Saturday is fair and cold. So I am quite confident that when we fly over that area the valley will be plainly visible from the air." He led the way into the living room and his wife dutifully followed, a piece of cake clutched firmly in one plump hand.

"No, Jenny," he said, just as though she had been arguing with him. "My mind is made up. The first reconnaissance flight shall take place on Saturday morning. After that we may have several days of inclement weather when the valley will be hidden from view." He sank into the nearest chair and began to suck on his pipe. "I know I am old and eccentric, but I cannot put off viewing that valley from the air any longer than is necessary."

"I don't blame you," Vicki cried impulsively. "I'd give my eyeteeth to go along with you."

"Me too." Mrs. Hyacith sighed. "Especially since the understanding with the three share-the-flighters is that if they should locate the valley on the reconnaissance flight and Max thinks they can land, they will. Even if it's only for an hour." She appealed to Vicki. "Under the circumstances, don't you think Hy should let me go with them on Saturday? I hate to miss the chance of being one of the first pioneers."

"I cannot permit you to accompany us without another woman passenger, Jenny," her husband said firmly.

"I wish you needed the services of a stewardess," Vicki said, thinking out loud. "I have Saturday off, and—"

"Vicki!" Mrs. Hyacith screeched at the top of her lungs, clutching Vicki, cake and all in her plump arms. "*YOU* shall be my chaperon."

Vicki managed a smothered giggle. "Or vice versa, Mrs. Hyacith. Anyway, let's persuade your husband to let us both go."

"I doubt very much if Lewis Barr would approve of my taking his daughter on what the rest of the world deems such a foolhardy venture," the professor began.

"Oh, gosh, sir!" It was Max coming to the women's rescue. "It's nothing more than a picnic. Vicki ought to see the Alaska Range from the air. And I'd like to have her company. I mean, I'd like to have a stewardess along just in case. What I really mean is, Mrs. Hyacith wants like anything to come along, and so—"

The professor held up a thin, blue-veined hand. "You have convinced me, young man. Your powers of persuasion could not be matched by that of some of our politicians." He chuckled silently. "As you say, it's to be nothing more than a picnic, and whoever heard of a picnic without womenfolk and ants?"

▓▓▓▓▓▓▓▓▓▓▓▓▓▓▓▓▓▓▓▓▓▓▓▓▓▓▓▓▓

CHAPTER III

Crash Landing

THE ATTRACTIVE YOUNG BUSH PILOT, MAX LOWLER, took Vicki back to her hotel after the Hyaciths' little dinner party.

"Let's have brunch tomorrow," he said. "You and I'll be the crew on that reconnaissance flight day after tomorrow. We should discuss weather, routes, and personalities of the passengers."

Vicki pretended to pout. "Are you going to make me work on my free day?"

He grinned. "Certainly not. But any excuse to see you before you go on duty tomorrow. After brunch, I'll talk you into having dinner with me tomorrow evening in Juneau. I'm flying back myself around noon."

Vicki thought for a moment. She liked Max and wanted to hear more about his checkered career. According to Mrs. Hyacith, he had flown over every inch of Alaska many times.

"Which is a large order," she had told Vicki earlier, "considering that Alaska is about one-fifth the size of the rest of the United States. Before he became an air-borne game warden he raised huskies, and in-between times made a living as a salmon fisherman. He was left an orphan at the ripe old age of twelve and soon learned to shift for himself very well. We met him once during the moose-hunting season, which Hy, of course, does with a camera, and never 'bags' anything because he can't remember to turn the film ahead after each picture. But Max is a crack shot as well as an excellent pilot."

"He looks as though he could do almost anything he set his mind to," Vicki reflected now as they stood in the hotel lobby waiting for the elevator. "And although I won't have the responsibility of a manifest on Saturday, I would like to know more about the personalities of the passengers."

Aloud she said with a smile, "The answer to both invitations is, Yes, thank you very much. I have to be aboard my ship before eleven tomorrow, so we'd better make it breakfast instead of brunch."

"Swell," he said. "I'll pick you up right here at eight. I know a place where we can get the best waffles in the world, smothered in sausages and maple sirup."

He was waiting for her when Vicki came down the next morning. She was wearing her uniform and had set the trim cap at a perky angle over her ash-blond hair.

"Boy, are you ever efficient looking," he said, his dark eyes teasing and admiring her at the same time. "And to show you how efficient I am, here's an informal passenger list complete with hints on how to handle the three other passengers."

Vicki took the scribbled notes, pretending it was a real manifest, and said, "How do you happen to know so much about them?"

He grinned mischievously. "When I left you here last night they were all three mysterious Messrs. X to me, but I always keep a promise. So I got their addresses from Mrs. Hyacith and called on each and every one between the hours of ten and midnight."

They took a cab to the famous Maison Blanc, which, Max told her, was known as "The Place Where Epicureans Meet." It was located in an old residence on a steep downtown hill.

"My goodness," Vicki gasped as Max helped her climb out of the taxi, "this hill is as bad as any in San Francisco. I'm glad I'm wearing sensible shoes."

"Down below us," he said, "is the water front which is known as the Alaskan Way. After breakfast I'll take you to 'Ivar's Acres of Clams.'"

"I couldn't eat clams at this time of the morning," Vicki protested when they were seated at a table. "And certainly not acres of them right after waffles."

"That's why I wanted to take you to brunch," he said. "No sight-seeing tour of Seattle would be complete without your meeting the ballad singer of

Puget Sound. So whether you can eat clams or not, we'll have to stop in at Ivar's. When he sees you, I know he'll break out his battered guitar and serenade us. And you'll love his place. It's right on the dock and is decorated with fish nets and all sorts of clam-digging equipment."

"Quite different from this restaurant, I imagine," Vicki said, admiring the murals which depicted scenes of old Paris and of Seattle in the days when Washington was still a territory.

Max chuckled. "Nevertheless, Ivar's slogan is 'Where Clams and Culture Meet.' He's a fascinating character. And while you're absorbing clams or culture, there may be a fire in the harbor. The fireboat dock is separated from Ivar's by just a small strip of water, so you won't miss any of the excitement."

Vicki smiled. "Ivar's is definitely the next stop. But now that we're in the midst of epicureans, what would you suggest that I order instead of good old-fashioned orange juice?"

"Onion soup," he said promptly, "complete with toasted croutons and cheese. It's the Maison Blanc's specialty."

As they waited for the delicious smelling soup to cool, Vicki said, "Before we discuss the three mysterious Messrs. X, Max, I'd like to know more about you. Mrs. Hyacith gave me a thumbnail sketch of your career last evening. You grew up in Alaska, didn't you?"

"That's right," he said. "I spent most of my child-

hood listening for the toot of a boat whistle, which meant we'd have good food for a change. Shipping and weather, you'll soon find out, are the two most important topics of conversation to any Alaskan, even a kid. On the rare days when the sun shone I'd play hooky from school because at other times it was too wet for football and baseball. And the mosquitoes in summer ruined the hunting and fishing. You have to wear gloves and a head net; also, believe it or not, the heat is suffocating." He chuckled. "But the coming of spring makes up for all other weather hazards. It arrives with a magic rush and the snow melts overnight. Suddenly everything is green, birds are singing and flowers burst into bloom like little jack-in-the-boxes. There was never any school on the first day of spring, and that was the best part of it all."

"And you could play baseball at midnight on the Fourth of July," Vicki added with a smile.

"That's right," he agreed. "Gosh, I feel sorry for kids who didn't grow up in Alaska. Why, I had my own husky pup to train when I was eight and could shoot and fish almost as well as my father when I was ten. Lucky for me that he taught me so much, because not long after that I had to support myself."

"You were about the same age as my sister Ginny," Vicki said softly, thinking that it must have been awfully hard for a boy of twelve to be left alone in the world. "How old were you when you

went into the business of breeding and training huskies?"

"Fifteen," he said with a rueful grin. "I didn't make much money, but I had a lot of fun. Contrary to popular opinion, huskies can be affectionate and make swell pets. The Indians, Eskimos, and old sourdoughs are convinced that they must never be shown any affection, and that they won't work unless they are fed only at the end of the trail. They rarely give them individual pet names, and most of their dogs answer to the one word, mush, which is derived from the French word, *marchons*. It can mean giddap or scram, depending on the owner's mood. Boy, oh boy, did Mordy and I have an argument about huskies last night!"

"Mordy?" Vicki asked in surprise. "Do you mean the old prospector, Mr. Mordecaw?"

He nodded. "And what a character that old buzzard is! Luckily I called on him last, otherwise I'd never have got around to seeing the other two. He talked my ear off."

"Wait a minute," Vicki interrupted. "What excuse did you give for calling on three complete strangers, anyway?"

"As the pilot, madam," he told her with mock severity, "I'm the captain of our little expedition. I won't be in Seattle again before the take-off tomorrow, so what was more natural than that I should rout them out of bed to tell them how they should outfit themselves? My old crate is heated, but sup-

pose we run into weather and have to make an emergency landing? Sleeping bags and blanket rolls would come in handy then."

"Don't be silly," Vicki said with a giggle. "I shouldn't think I'd have to remind *you* of the strict Alaskan law concerning emergency equipment that is required per person in every plane." She began to count on her fingers, "Snowshoes, sleeping bag, concentrated food rations, matches in waterproof container, flashlight, insect repellent, compass, ax, rifle, ammunition, and fishing tackle. Furthermore, before we leave Anchorage we'll know if there's any chance of running into weather, and if so, the flight will be postponed, won't it?"

"Natch," he agreed, "but it served as a good excuse. Frankly, I was as curious about those three passengers as you were."

"And still am," Vicki added. "Max, do you think there's any chance that we'll locate that valley tomorrow?"

"I do," he said. "According to old Mordy, it isn't far as the crow flies from Rainy Pass. And since the professor seems to feel sure it won't be blanketed with mist at this time of the year, we should be able to find it without too much difficulty."

"And if we do," Vicki went on, "you're going to try to land?"

He nodded. "If it's at all possible to set down my crate on the valley floor, I think we should. If only long enough to let the professor gather some proof

of its existence. Then the university will undoubtedly finance a scientific expedition. The Hyaciths haven't much money, you know. He can't afford many share-the-flight trips."

Vicki nodded. "And I suppose the others feel the same way about landing if we can. It won't take the engineer long to make a brief survey for his firm, and the author could take a lot of notes in an hour. But unless he has phenomenal luck, even with a Geiger counter, the prospector can't hope to find uranium right away."

"Oh, they'll all want to come back," Max said. "But I wouldn't be surprised if Mordy decided to stay. That is, if the valley is warm enough for him to survive the winter. En route to the Klondike in the winter of '98, he traveled by shanks' mare to White Pass summit. After living through that, a hot springs valley will probably seem like a steam-heated apartment to him."

Vicki frowned thoughtfully. "He must be an old man now, and even if he doesn't mind the cold, what is he going to eat?"

"That's the least of his worries," Max said. "From the bird's-eye view he got of the place, he probably knows that there are squirrels and undoubtedly fish in the stream."

"My goodness," Vicki exclaimed. "He really did get a good look at it, didn't he?"

"Apparently," Max said, and added quietly, "I

don't know whether to believe half of what he says or none of it. And frankly, I'm going to see to it that all three of those men pay their share in advance. I'm not going to have Hy left holding the bag."

Vicki's blue eyes widened with surprise. "Then you don't really trust any of them?"

"It's not that," he told her quickly. "I know enough about engineering to be sure Chapman is the real McCoy, and Brossard seems like a nice enough fellow. But what do we really know about any of them?"

"But surely, Max," Vicki protested, "Professor Hyacith asked for references."

Max sighed. "He may have asked for them and he may have got them, but he didn't do any checking. He and Jenny accept everybody at face value anyway, and I don't think they've ever been stung." He shrugged. "It really doesn't matter as long as the others pay in advance, and I can handle that end of it in Anchorage."

"You don't trust them," Vicki said again.

"All right, then," he admitted as he helped her into her coat, "I don't. And now for a bird's-eye view of Seattle from the Chinese Room in the Smith Tower. It's only a short walk from there to Ivar's."

Sure enough, the famous ballad singer did serenade them. And the lyrics to his song kept reminding Vicki of "Mordy," the old prospector.

"I've traveled all over this country
Prospecting and digging for gold,
I've tunneled, hydraulicked, and cradled
And I have been frequently sold.

So rolling my grub in a blanket
I left all my tools on the ground,
And started one morning to shank it
For a country they called Puget Sound.

Arriving flat broke in midwinter
I found it enveloped in fog,
And covered all over with timber
Thick as hair on the back of a dog."

Listening, Vicki stared out at the boats in the bay. If they found the valley and landed tomorrow, the picnic might well turn out to be an exciting adventure. Aloud she said to Max:

"I hope that when we fly over it tomorrow the valley won't be enveloped in fog."

"And I," he said, grinning, "since I'm determined to land, hope it won't be 'covered all over with timber.'"

Later, flying high above clouds in the big Federal plane en route to Juneau, Vicki found time from her duties to glance at the scribbled notes Max had given her that morning.

"Blair Brossard," she read. "Tall and blond, but not nearly as handsome as I am, Vic! A typical dreamy-eyed novelist, almost feverishly excited

about the flight. If you fall for him while I'm up front tomorrow, I'll wreck the plane. He lives in a moderately priced, inexpensively furnished apartment in Seattle.

"Alec Chapman. Must be a topflight engineer, for he lives in the penthouse of a de luxe apartment hotel. Would say that he's used to having plenty of money and spends it freely. He would not divulge the name of the firm he is representing. His reason: If the valley turns out to be a myth, the boss doesn't want it bruited about that they were investigating it. Medium height, stocky build, in his middle thirties. I guess you'd call him sophisticated.

"Mordy Mordecaw. Wow! Must have once been a magnificent physical specimen, and even now is as hard as nails and as spry as a grasshopper. Claims he was barely out of his teens and living in Seattle when he caught the Klondike fever in '97. You'll like him in spite of the fact that he never quite looks into your eyes. This is probably not due to a shifty nature, but to the fact that he may well have lost the sight of one eye sometime or other during his adventurous life."

"He sounds delightful," Vicki decided as she hurried down the aisle in answer to a passenger's signal. "I don't care whether he has shifty eyes or not!"

Late that afternoon she finished buying souvenirs in the Nugget Shop on Juneau's narrow main street. The presents she picked out were mostly products of Indian handicraft. Sweet-smelling sewing baskets

for her mother, Mrs. Duff, and Charmion Wilson. For the other flight stewardesses who shared the New York apartment with her she chose dainty, beaded moccasins.

"Jean and Dot," she reflected, "will wear 'em with slacks, and the white ones I got for Tessa and Celia will go nicely with their glamorous housecoats."

Ginny's present was a bottle of perfume, shaped like a gold nugget. It took Vicki a long time to pick out a suitable gift for her father. She usually sent him something that was more of a joke than a present, and finally decided upon a gaily feathered headdress.

"To don in place of your chef's cap," she wrote on the gift card, "when Mother goes on the warpath after you've messed up her kitchen!"

Max was waiting for her outside the shop, standing between the tall totem poles. They strolled down the street to the Baronof Hotel, where, he said, they could get a delicious dinner.

"Speaking of totems," he said, "we should pick out an animal or plant as our own totem for the flight tomorrow. What will you have? Animal or vegetable, fish or fowl?"

"Steak," Vicki said promptly. "My favorite food."

"Reindeer or moose?" he came right back at her.

"Reindeer," she said after a moment, "because we're not too, too far from Santa Claus's domain."

"Which one?" he demanded. "Comet or Cupid? Donder or Blitzen?"

"Vixen," Vicki said almost without thinking. "We women are going to be badly enough outnumbered by men as it is."

He stopped in front of the hotel to stare down at her. "You're psychic! Long, long before I ever knew Professor and Mrs. Barr had a very pretty daughter named Vicki, I christened my winged ferryboat The Vixen."

They held hands then, laughing and chanting together:

"To the top of the porch,
To the top of the wall,
Now dash away, dash away, dash away ALL!"

Then, almost before Vicki could believe it, Max's Vixen, with her six eager passengers and pilot, was soaring above Anchorage, on her way to a fabulous valley in the Alaska Range. The trim ship seemed to be almost alive as they took to the air, prancing and pawing for altitude until Max leveled her off. When she settled down to a more matronly pace, Vicki glanced around at her fellow passengers.

Mrs. Hyacith was busily inspecting the contents of the enormous picnic basket and thermos jug she had brought along "just in case someone should get hungry." Her husband had hopelessly entangled his shoulder camera gear with his seat belt and was vainly plucking at the various straps.

Vicki hastened to extricate him.

"Only a Houdini like me could get him out of that

strait jacket," a gruff voice behind her said. Gnarled brown hands reached over her shoulders and in half a minute the stubby fingers had set the professor free.

Without turning or looking up, Vicki knew that those clumsy-looking but deft hands belonged to Mordy Mordecaw. She stayed there with her head bent until he had returned to his seat, for she didn't yet dare look at him without bursting into gales of laughter.

Just before the take-off the eyes of everyone at the airport, and especially Vicki's, had almost popped out of their heads when the old prospector arrived on the scene. He looked like a tall, thin Santa Claus, and slung over one shoulder was a pack which Vicki felt sure must contain a tent, poncho, two fur-lined parkas, and several pounds of sourdough. Pulled down over his ears was a moth-eaten ermine cap which matched his loose-fitting jacket and baggy trousers. White rabbit's fur mittens and boots completed the ensemble.

It was a clear, cold day and the ground was covered with hard-packed snow, so they were all dressed warmly and were wearing galoshes or rubber boots. "But Mordy," Vicki whispered to Max, "looks as though we weren't going to stop until we reach the North Pole."

"He sure does," Max had agreed. "And I can't imagine why he had to pick an unpractical color like white. If he must play Santa Claus and 'dress

all in fur from his head to his feet' you'd think he'd choose one that wouldn't show every speck of 'ashes and soot.' "

Now that they were in the heated plane, flying high above billowing clouds, Vicki was sure that Mordy must be sweltering. Slowly she straightened and, with her lips pressed tightly together to keep from laughing, turned in the old prospector's direction. What she saw made her mouth fall open, try as she did to keep it clamped shut. Now he had emerged from his fur cocoon and was garbed in the formless costume of a deep-sea diver. To make the picture even more ludicrous, he was reading, with obvious difficulty, whatever was written on a soiled piece of paper which he held close to his nose.

Before Vicki could regain her poise, he looked up to find her staring at him. "Map," he said succinctly. "Drawed it myself." And then, realizing that it was his change of costume which was making her stare at him, he grinned. "Pertection against merskiters. Them critters can stick their beaks right through wool, but this here garment is made of foam rubber. They gotta sting through layers and layers before they'll git me."

Vicki swallowed hard and said, "But isn't it awfully hot?"

He shrugged his bony shoulders. "Smart thing to do is keep the heat in when you got it. Now, I recall oncet when I was campin' alongside the Thirtymile River—"

He launched into a lurid description then of the hardships he had endured while climbing mountains of ice, stumbling through blizzards, half-frozen, and on the verge of starving. All for the sake of gold which he inevitably abandoned shortly before luckier and later sourdoughs found it in abundance in the very same spot.

Vicki and the other passengers listened enthralled.

"If only I'd of hung on a bit longer," he mourned reminiscently. "Had a rich claim on El Dorado and another on Bonanza, but no money in my poke, so I had to sell 'em to a hydraulic outfit that ended up takin' a hundred grand a year outta them ditches."

At the word "hydraulic," everyone looked at Mr. Chapman who nodded understandingly. "I imagine Mr. Mordecaw's difficulty was an insufficient volume of water to wash off the gravel in his sluice box."

"Volume?" The old Yukoner snorted. "When the snow had done meltin' there wasn't no water a-tall. Nary a drop."

Just then Max's voice came crackling over the loud-speaker. "We're nearing the general radius of our destination. According to my calculations we should fly over the valley within the next hour. Will you all please man the binoculars?"

There was a general flurry of excitement and then a tense silence as they all peered down intently at snow-clad mountains. Those very mountains, Vicki

knew, with their treacherous updrafts and downdrafts, would prevent Max from flying any lower.
Suddenly she decided that the whole expedition was
futile. From this altitude they might crisscross
above the valley a dozen times without catching the
faintest glimpse of it. She was on the verge of tuck-
ing her instrument back in its case when it dawned
on her that they were now flying above a vast mountain plateau, rolling out whitely between the mam-
moth peaks.

At the same moment, Max began to bring the
Vixen down.

"It's gotta be dead ahead of us," the old prospector cackled excitedly. "Dead ahead."

The plateau thinned out into what Vicki felt was
a dangerously thin white ribbon between two
mountains. Then all of a sudden it wasn't a plateau
any more, it was a mile-wide veil of mist.

"This must be it," Max yelled over the intercom.

"This *is* it!" Professor Hyacith's normally quiet
voice was a shout of triumph, for just then the veil
lifted, as though giant fingers had torn it apart.

Vicki held her breath and blinked as she stared
down. Up until that moment she hadn't really believed they would find the valley, if there was one.
And now, there it was, lush and green, with a
sparkling waterfall cascading from a shelf halfway
up one cliff down into a rippling stream on the floor.

Max had dropped the Vixen's nose now and was
turning to come back, losing altitude all the time.

Vicki couldn't help wondering if perhaps he had been caught in a downdraft. Surely he wouldn't attempt to land in that narrow valley with its small clearing.

But down he came and the passengers began to fasten their seat belts.

"I can't believe it," Mrs. Hyacith chortled over and over again.

Mr. Chapman stammered something unintelligible and Vicki glanced swiftly at him in surprise. Up until then he'd seemed so blasé, as though he, for one, did not really believe the valley existed. Vicki had got the impression that he was bored with the whole trip, that this was all in a day's work to him. But now she began to wonder. He was peering down through his binoculars, mumbling and muttering to himself, obviously as excited as the rest of them.

Her eyes traveled on to the face of the young novelist. He was sitting there, bug-eyed, gnawing his lower lip until Vicki was sure it would bleed any minute. Sharing the same seat was Mr. Mordecaw, bug-eyed too, and clawing at the air beneath his chin.

"I'll bet he had a beard not too long ago," Vicki decided, and then thought no more about it, for just then the Vixen touched ground with a violent jolt and careened wildly along the narrow clearing between the stream and the wooded area that edged the west wall.

The minute her wheels stopped rolling, the passengers were out of their seats, everyone talking at once. In another few minutes Max was there in the aisle too, his face white beneath his tan.

"Quiet, all of you," he shouted above the uproar. "We're here all right, but I'm afraid we're here to stay for a long time. The radio isn't working and the plane must have hit a rock or a tree stump which I couldn't see from the air. From the way she behaved after that, I'm pretty sure the tail wheel was ripped off."

All Vicki could think of at that moment were those sheer, unscalable canyon walls soaring above the narrow floor of the valley. The horrified silence that followed Max's announcement was broken by the old prospector who calmly opened the door and peered out.

"You sure have lost your tail wheel, young feller," he told the pilot cheerfully. "And my guess is that her whole underside is out of kilter." He grinned widely, displaying uneven rows of tobacco-yellowed teeth. "You got good control of your nerves, boy; otherwise we might of cracked up and all been kilt."

Max forced a smile to his taut lips. "I thought sure we were going to for the longest minute I ever lived through."

Mr. Mordecaw hopped nimbly down to the ground. "Well, now," he said happily, "it'll be quite a spell before we're rescued. Guess maybe I'll strike uranium by then."

Professor Hyacith joined him, muttering glee-fully, "What unlooked-for good fortune! I'll have several days in which to gather specimens."

Vicki was still so dazed she hardly realized that Mr. Chapman had pushed roughly past her to the entrance.

"You fools!" he shouted hysterically to the two older men. "You blithering idiots! Look up at the sky. What do you see? Nothing but mist, white cottony mist! No one's going to rescue us. No one can find us. We're trapped, do you hear? TRAPPED!"

CHAPTER IV

A Quarrel

LITTLE PRICKLES OF FEAR CREPT UP VICKI'S SPINE. MR. Chapman was probably right. The mist might not lift again for weeks. Even then it might lift and close in again just before or right after a rescue plane flew over that spot.

"For goodness sake, Vicki Barr!" It was Mrs. Hyacith's loud voice that dragged Vicki back to the present. "Don't stand there as though we had nothing to do. Help me set out this food. Thank heavens I had the presence of mind to bring a whole stuffed turkey, five pounds of potato salad, three bunches of sliced carrots and a gallon of coffee, not to mention two dozen cupcakes and a lemon meringue pie. At least we won't starve."

Vicki laughed in spite of her worries. But the young novelist whirled on the professor's wife, white-lipped and tense. "You don't seem to understand," he cried jerkily. "We may be here for months, forever. Why, you're as silly as that woman

53

in *The Peterkin Papers*. When she thought they were snowed in, she got up the whole family before dawn and made them eat every bit of food in the house because she was afraid they'd never get any more."

Mrs. Hyacith laughed good-naturedly. "Calm down, son, and keep a civil tongue in your head. I'm not as rattlebrained as Mrs. Peterkin. But I do happen to know that nothing soothes one's nerves like a good, wholesome meal. Here, gnaw on this drumstick and leave your knuckles alone. You'll need your hands pretty soon, because we'll all have to pitch in and build some sort of a shelter before night sets in."

"You're right, Jenny," Max said. "Mr. Chapman, Mr. Brossard, and I can make two tents out of parachutes. It's sure to be damp and cold at night unless we get under cover."

The engineer, who had been staring moodily up at the veil of mist that hung so low it hid the top of the waterfall from view, wheeled to face Max.

"Why in the name of heaven do you all have to be so cheerful? This isn't a picnic. I don't know and I don't care about the rest of you. But *I've* got to get out of here, and fast."

"Then git," old Mr. Mordecaw said dryly as he accepted from Vicki a paper plate heaped high with food. "I suppose you're figgerin' on makin' wings out of the 'chutes on the theory that what goes down must come up, eh?"

Mr. Chapman's face flamed with anger. Before he could say a word, Mrs. Hyacith pushed him down on the grass and plopped a plate on his lap. "Eat," she commanded. "What do you think I'm running, a dog wagon where you can get food whenever it strikes your fancy? When I dish out, folks eat, if they don't, they wait until the next meal. You're acting like a spoiled child, and I'll bet you were brought up by a nurse who was paid to cater to your whims."

He stared up at her in the defiant manner of a little boy caught with jam all over his face. "It's none of your business, but I *was* brought up by nurses and governesses, which is the only civilized way to bring up children."

"Then act civilized," Mrs. Hyacith said, turning away from him as though he were beneath her notice.

Mr. Brossard, whom she had already intimidated into good behavior, said to the young engineer, "Say, if you had nurses and governesses, you must be a rich man's son. Are you by any chance related to the McKelvy Chapmans? She's one of our best customers." He stopped suddenly and bit his lip, a chagrined expression on his face.

"Oh," Vicki said quietly. "Then you have a job and write nights, Mr. Brossard?"

"Yes, I do," he said evenly. "How do you suppose I eat?"

"I didn't mean to be inquisitive," Vicki said pla-

catingly. "I was just thinking that we're both in the same boat. You're expected back to work on Monday, and I'm supposed to go on duty tomorrow morning. I'm worried about that, because I'm a flight stewardess and there isn't anybody to take my place. It means somebody who has a free day tomorrow will have to give it up."

"I should think that would be the least of your worries," Mr. Chapman said sourly.

Vicki ignored him. "Where do you work, Mr. Brossard?" she asked. "Will it upset things when you don't show up Monday morning?"

"It's none of your business where I work," he said in a surly tone of voice.

"Well, it's some of my business," Mrs. Hyacith put in emphatically. "When you interviewed my husband and me in answer to our ad, you stated definitely that you had no job and that's why you couldn't give your boss as a reference."

He stared morosely at the lemon meringue pie before replying. Then he blurted, "Oh, why do people have to be so nosy? The simple truth of the matter is that I did have a job, but I quit recently in order to devote all my time to my novel."

"Quit," Mr. Chapman sneered. "If you'd resigned you still could have used your firm as a reference. Why don't you admit you were fired? You don't look smart enough to hold down a job very long in a place my mother would patronize."

It was Mr. Brossard's turn to sneer. "So the rich Mrs. McKelvy Chapman is your mother, huh? If so, what are you doing here with us poor but honest people? With all that money, I should think you'd have a plane of your own."

The engineer's face turned red, then white, then red again. For a minute Vicki thought he was going to throw his plate of food at the young novelist.

"Oh, let's all stop prying," she said in a mollified tone of voice. "It's all my fault. My insatiable curiosity started it. What difference can it make in this valley whether any of us is rich or poor?"

"That's not the point," Mr. Chapman told her coldly. "The point is, are we all honest?"

"Well, you for one," Mrs. Hyacith put in tartly, "came with us under false colors. Why didn't you use your father's name as a reference? He's one of the trustees of the university." She pursed her lips. "Hy and I know him very well."

Viciously he mashed a slice of potato to pulp, and then burst out with, "I'm thirty-five years old, Mrs. Hyacith. Don't you think it's time I tried getting along without my father's name?"

"You're perfectly right," she said, instantly contrite. And then, Vicki guessed, in order to change the subject, she said jokingly, "Oh, dear, Hy's disappeared as usual just when I've put food on his plate. He's probably wandered right into the mouth of a Kodiak bear and isn't aware of it yet."

Suddenly the tension broke. Everyone laughed except Mr. Brossard whose bright blue eyes darted worriedly around the clearing.

"Why, Professor Hyacith *has* disappeared," he muttered, more to himself than to the others. "I'd better go and look for him at once." Then, as he realized that his solicitous attitude was making Vicki frown at him with a puzzled expression on her face, he added hastily, "After all, he *may* have met up with a bear."

"No bears here," Mr. Mordecaw said with a chuckle. "I could smell 'em if there was. But plenty of pack rats, I'll warrant. Bet there's an army of them varmints sittin' at the edge of the woods right now, waitin' for night to fall so they can start in tradin' with us. If you got anythin' bright and shiny, folks, best put it under your sleepin' bags tonight. Why," he went on, warming to his subject, "pack rats is worse than magpies and jays. A buddy of mine oncet, who slept with his mouth open, woke up and found all his gold fillin's gone. And what do you think them thievin' little critters left in trade?"

"False teeth," Vicki said promptly, laughing.

"And that ain't no lie," the old prospector said, giving her an admiring glance. "False choppers that'd been swiped from a feller in the next tent."

"This is no laughing matter," the young novelist broke in seriously, too seriously, Vicki thought. "It's important," he informed them all curtly, "that from now on no one wanders off by himself without first

telling the others his route and his destination."

"Ho, ho," Jenny interrupted. "Try and make Hy obey that rule! He came here to find the hot springs and some old bones. He'll never have any idea of his route and destination until he finds them."

Mr. Brossard glared at her. "I cannot understand how you can sit there placidly. Your husband may well be in serious trouble right now. I shall go and look for him." He started off into the woods at a fast trot.

"Well, I never," Jenny exploded. "Since when did that selfish young man grow so found of Hy that now he must play nursemaid to him?"

"And," Vicki added, "what makes him think he's going to lay down rules and regulations for us all to follow? That's Max's job." She glanced swiftly around the clearing. "Why, where *is* Max? He was right beside me a second ago, wolfing down his food."

"Here I am, Vic," he said, sticking his head out of a window in the plane. He beckoned her to come inside. "I've been trying to figure things out and have come to the sad conclusion that acid is leaking out of the storage-battery case which must have been cracked when we hit. No lights and the radio is dead. But the worst part of it is, that even if we could repair the Vixen's undercarriage, we couldn't get out of here."

Vicki nodded. "It's a pretty small clearing."

"That's right," he said ruefully. "I knew it would

be a tight squeeze when I brought her down, but in the excitement of the moment I forgot that the higher you are above sea level the more runway you need for a take-off. The point is that search planes aren't going to make the same mistake I did. Even if we could signal to them, they wouldn't take the risk I did."

"But, Max," Vicki interrupted, "a helicopter could land here and take off, couldn't it?"

"Sure," he said unenthusiastically. "But since we can't signal that fact to the outside world, no helicopters are going to be flying above us. If I hadn't been looking for this valley I would have taken it for granted that the cream-sauce mist above us was simply an extension of the plateau."

"I see," Vicki said thoughtfully. "If only we could attract the attention of one of the planes that should be trying to locate us pretty soon, the pilot might fly low enough to figure out that we are in a valley under a veil of fog, and send a helicopter to the rescue."

He shrugged. "If, from where I sit, is the biggest word in the English language."

"We've still got our flashlights," Vicki pointed out. "I've heard pilots say that at night they can see a lighted cigarette a mile above the ground."

"But," Max objected, "nobody's going to be flying above this area at night. It's too risky. The up- and downdrafts on both sides of the mountains are tricky enough in the daytime."

Suddenly Vicki had an idea. "How about a sail-plane, Max? If we could build a glider and launch it from that slope over there, wouldn't a thermal carry it up and over one of the mountains?"

"You're a mind reader," he said approvingly. "That's what I've been leading up to. It's our only hope, anyway. A thousand feet above us the temperature is ten below zero. Sooner or later it's going to seep into this valley and counteract the effect of the hot springs. We've got to get out before that happens."

Vicki stared at the small slope of land near the southern wall. Even if they could build a glider, would they be able to launch it? "You know, Max," she said soberly, "I'm awfully afraid we're in for a siege of nerves. It's going to drive some people almost out of their minds when they hear those rescue planes flying above us but cut off from view by the veil of mist."

Max nodded. "By some people I guess you mean Brossard and Chapman. Chapman sounds a little nuts right now. Wonder why he's in such a darned hurry to get out?"

"Maybe he can't bear the thought of the anxiety it'll cause his parents," Vicki said slowly. "As a matter of fact, I've been keeping my fingers crossed ever since that first jolt, inwardly praying that Federal won't let mine know that I'm lost somewhere in the Alaska Range. Do you think the airline will, Max?"

He smiled down at her small, worried face. "Not

right away, Vic. If there were any signs of a wrecked plane, then of course they would. But we're known to have adequate emergency equipment, and, as Jenny would say, 'if I do say so myself,' I've got a pretty good reputation for getting out of difficulties. So I doubt if your family will be notified before we're out of here."

Vicki's tense features relaxed. "Then you think we really will be able to get out by glider?"

"Well, we've got to try it," he said, "if for no other reason than that a community project is generally a good morale booster. If we can find the right kind of wood, building a sailplane shouldn't take more than a few days. That is, if Chapman and Brossard will help."

"I'd count on the engineer," Vicki said. "But not on the novelist. There's something about Mr. Brossard that doesn't quite ring true to me—several things, in fact."

"That's good," Max said cheerfully. "Keep on with that attitude. So far as I'm concerned, the only thing wrong with him is that he's just a little too good-looking. Chapman's the one I don't feel happy about. What's his hurry, anyway, and why didn't he use his father's name as a reference?"

"That," Vicki said, "doesn't bother me as much as Mr. Brossard's evasiveness about his job which he had and now hasn't. And then the way he suddenly changed from a sulky little boy and became ter- ribly, terribly concerned about the professor's wel-

fare. Why, even Mrs. Hyacith was surprised."

"I must have been tinkering with the radio when that happened," Max said. "What's happened to Hy?"

"I doubt if anything has happened to him," Vicki said. "He simply wandered off into the woods. Nobody, not even his wife, was worried, but our novelist insisted upon dashing off in search of him as though Professor Hyacith were his bosom friend." She sighed. "And just before he made himself a one-man search party, he laid down some strict rules and regulations which I, for one, have no intention of obeying. This is my holiday, stolen though it may be." She laughed. "When I'm working I'm either always on duty or have to notify the airline where I can be reached. I'll be darned if I'm going to report to Mr. Brossard every time I leave the clearing."

Max threw back his head, roaring with laughter. "You and me both. Since when did he appoint himself captain of the camp? Who does he think he is, Robinson Crusoe?"

"That's another point," Vicki said seriously. "If I were writing a book and had just escaped sudden death in a crash landing in a fabulous valley, I'd be delighted with the whole setup. Why, Max, this adventure is all he needs to make his book a bestseller. But what does he do? Take notes so he won't risk forgetting his and the other passengers reactions to the accident? No, instead he was practically

insulting to Mrs. Hyacith who at that moment was striving against all odds to keep him and Mr. Chapman from going to pieces!"

"Well," Max said easily, "everybody was pretty much on edge at first. Once we've settled down to a routine, and work on the glider has started, I think—"

A loud voice at the door interrupted: "A time and place for everything, you two! This may be the place but it's not the time for romance." It was Mrs. Hyacith, grinning broadly. "Hy just wandered back," she told them. "And would you believe it? He's already located the hot springs and is as pleased as punch with himself."

"And," Vicki asked curiously, "did Mr. Brossard locate *him?*"

"Of course not," Mrs. Hyacith said with a sniff. "How could a tenderfoot like that even think for a minute that he could find anyone in those woods? So now *he's* missing, and so far as I'm concerned, that bossy individual can stay lost, *after* we've built the tents. Mordy offered to go look for him, in fact insisted upon it, which surprised me, because I don't think that old pack rat is any fonder of our young novelist than I am." She sighed. "And I must say, if we're going to spend all our time looking for each other, we'll get nowhere fast."

Vicki glanced out of the nearest window. "Here they both come now, looking as pleased with each other as two dogs with but one bone. From the ex-

pression on Mr. Brossard's face I'd say that he wanted to stay lost."

"That's exactly what I was thinking," Mrs. Hyacith said from the door. "But we can't waste time worrying about what makes that one tick. I've given the paper plates a lick and a promise, Vicki, so will you gather up the silver and wash it in the stream? MAX!" she boomed. "Get out the parachutes and that sewing kit I gave you last Christmas. It'll be dark soon."

"Yes, ma'am," they both said together. Max added in a meek aside to Vicki: "There's room for the seven of us to spend this first night in the plane, but I wouldn't dare argue with Dame Rip Van Winkle, would you?"

Vicki shook her head. "And she's right. We must all try somehow to get a good night's sleep, which we wouldn't, stacked in here like sardines. Tomorrow, everyone's got to get out of the right side of his sleeping bag and be cheerful and co-operative."

With a gay smile Vicki hurried out of the plane to collect the eating utensils. But deep down inside her she didn't feel gay. No matter how well Mr. Chapman and Mr. Brossard slept that night she felt quite sure that they would not wake up in a cheerful, co-operative mood.

CHAPTER V

The Crown Jewels

VICKI'S WORST APPREHENSIONS CAME TRUE. THE building of parachute tents had taken longer than anyone expected. They had hardly been erected in a temporary way when the sunlight which filtered through the veil of mist was obliterated by the quick, long northern night.

Even Mrs. Hyacith had sighed with exasperation. "We shouldn't go to bed on empty stomachs," she complained. "But we can't afford to waste matches and flashlight batteries. Come on, Vic. Into the ladies' compartment for us. We'll have to grope our way into the silk and satin sleeping bags."

Vicki giggled. "I'm glad I'm not like the princess who couldn't sleep with a pea under her mattress. There're a couple of sharp little boulders under my downy couch."

"You should gain weight," Mrs. Hyacith said with a chuckle. "Like me. I could sleep on a porcupine

and not know it." And just like that, she was snoring peacefully.

Vicki had lain awake for a long time wondering about a lot of things. In the first place, although everyone else had pitched in and helped with the tents, old Mr. Mordecaw had flatly refused to have anything to do with that project.

"I'd get trophoclawstia in one of them things," he said, meaning, Vicki gathered, claustrophobia. "I've slept in the open during blizzards, so a little dew ain't goin' to give me pewnewmonia."

Mrs. Hyacith had glared at him as though she were going to rap him on the knuckles with her big gold thimble. "Then what *are* you going to do to be helpful, Mr. Mordecaw?" she demanded.

"And that reminds me, ma'am," he drawled. "Seein' as how we're all in this here place together where eddication don't matter, I'd sure appreciate it if you'd call me Mordy, and 'low me to call you by your given name. Jenny, ain't it? And a right nice monniker it is, for a fine, husky lass like you."

Her good humor completely restored, Mrs. Hyacith had beamed on him. "You're right, Mordy. Let's all call each other by our first names from now on. Does that suit you, Blair Brossard and Alec Chapman? I know Hy, Vicki, and Max will agree."

The engineer and the novelist had nodded without comment, and Mordy winked at Jenny. He looked so droll in his new outfit that Vicki could hardly keep from laughing. He had changed into a

loose-fitting brown and green suit that made him look like a tall, thin Brownie.

"Well, now, Jenny," he said, "I'll answer your question. I figgered that somebody ought to do some scoutin' before we settle down fer the night. Not that I'm afeared of wild beasts, mind you, but still and all, somethin' jest might be in them woods that's layin' low now, waitin' fer the dark, to come snoopin' around the camp. I don't aim to wake up with no moon shinin' and find a mountain goat eatin' my beard, I mean my—"

"When *did* you shave off your beard, Mordy?" Vicki asked quietly.

He turned toward her, but his eyes were focused on something behind her left shoulder. "Why, jist afore I made up my mind to go prospectin' for uranium, Vic," he said blandly. "Don't you know that it's downright dangerous to meander along in freezin' weather with a beard? The Eskermos, now, they don't have much more than a chin whisker or two to begin with, but they always pluck 'em out afore takin' a long walk in the snow."

"And quite intelligent of them too," Hy said with an approving nod. "The moisture of your own breath is apt to cling to the hairs on your face and freeze, forming a film of ice that is not easy to thaw out."

"That's right," Max added as he hammered a tent pole into the ground with the broad end of his ax-head. "And I think Mordy's right, too, to do a little

scouting before it gets pitch dark. Who knows, he might come back with a deer or a moose and then we could have a potlatch."

The old prospector promptly shouldered his rifle and started for the woods. "I aim to come back with somethin'," he said.

Vicki looked up from the tent flap she was sewing and watched him. One minute he was at the edge of the clearing, and the next, he had faded into the foliage. "So that's why he changed costumes," she thought. "And what perfect camouflage for hunting!"

Aloud she asked Max, "What's a potlatch?"

"An Indian festival," he told her, "that often lasts for days and days. It's sort of a community birthday party, generally in celebration of a wedding or an Indian maiden's debut. The proud father gives everyone a present."

"What a wonderful idea," Vicki said. And then in order to draw the silent members of the party into the general conversation, she proposed a game. "Let's pretend that Hy is going to give a potlatch. What would you like as a gift, Mr. Chapman—I mean, Alec?"

"Wings," he said without smiling.

"And you, Blair?"

"To be here alone," he muttered to the tent peg he was whittling. Then he added quickly, "Or at least some place where I could get away from silly questions asked by silly girls."

Vicki had laughed good-naturedly, but now, in the sifted sunlight of morning as she helped Jenny prepare breakfast, she couldn't help wondering why Blair Brossard was so consistently disagreeable to her. The strange part of it was that up until the moment when the old prospector had suggested his scouting expedition, the young novelist had been whistling cheerfully. Vicki had thought for a while that Max was right; routine, hard work had had its desired effect. Even the two surly members of the party had been enthusiastic when Max told them that he had found some saplings in the near-by woods which could be used in the building of a glider. And they had both worked like beavers helping erect the tents.

Until Mordy set off for the woods. After that Blair's hands had grown clumsy and he had remained grimly silent, stopping every now and then to stare at the spot where Mordy had faded into the foliage.

Suddenly Vicki was struck with an idea. "It isn't that Blair Brossard has taken a dislike to me," she decided. "It's just that he doesn't like the idea of any one of us going off by himself."

But why on earth should he care? she asked herself. An old sourdough like Mordy, especially since he was equipped with a gun, could certainly take care of himself.

And then her thoughts traveled to the whereabouts of the prospector. He had not returned when

she and Jenny had gone to bed. And in the morning there was a note impaled on the spit above a dying campfire saying:

"Hev et gon after moose. Mordy."

"The old fox has appointed himself the hunter of the party," Jenny told Vicki with a philosophical chuckle. "And it's just as well. He wouldn't be much help with the building of a glider."

"Why not?" Vicki asked, thinking out loud. "He can pilot a helicopter, which is some achievement. He must know something about what makes aircraft fly."

"Pooh," Jenny said, glaring resentfully at the sad-looking remains of her potato salad. "I never did believe that yarn. Do you suppose anyone will eat these things if I fry them?"

"I'm sure they'll be delicious," Vicki said. "But what are you going to fry them in?"

"A skillet, of course," Jenny told her airily and raised her voice. "Max, MAX!"

The young pilot emerged from the woods with an armful of kindling wood. "Ma'am?"

"Fetch me that battered old aluminum kitchenware you keep cached in the plane. Vicki'll need a pot to warm up the coffee and I need a frying pan."

"I'll get them," Vicki offered. "Just tell me where to look, Max."

"In the locker under the second seat on the starboard side," he said. "If you can't find the catch, give a yell."

"Aye, aye, sir." She hoisted herself into the plane. While she was looking for the catch that would release the seat that formed the top of the storage space, she saw a yellowed piece of paper on the floor.

"Somebody dropped something in the excitement of our jolting landing," she reflected, and reached down to pick it up. "Why, it's so old it's about to fall to pieces," she thought, hesitating for fear the thin sheet of folded paper might come apart at the creases when she touched it.

Could this be the map Mordy had been holding close to his nose yesterday in the plane when he had caught her staring at him in his odd-looking costume of foam rubber? Vicki remembered that after that he had kept them all enthralled with lurid descriptions of his adventures in the Klondike. She herself had been so interested in his yarns right up until they sighted the valley that now she could not remember what he had done with the map while he talked. Had the old man been so carried away by his own reminiscences that, without realizing it, he had let the map slip from his fingers to the floor of the plane? And then, in the excitement of the crash landing, had he forgotten all about it?

Now that they had reached the valley the map he had "drawed" himself was probably of no value, but he might want it back, anyway. Gingerly she picked it up, using both hands, and then she almost dropped it. It was not a map, it was a letter, and she

stared in amazement at a phrase a few lines below the heading.

The ink was faded and the penmanship that of the almost illegible, flowery scrawl fashionable in a long-forgotten era, but to Vicki the words "Tsar's jewels" stood out with startling clarity. Her eyes traveled of their own volition upward to the date, February 15th, 1881.

Then the tsar must have been Alexander II of Russia who sold Alaska to the United States in 1867! Vicki had learned to remember the date in school because six and seven were thirteen, and at the time of the purchase Alaska was jeeringly referred to as "Seward's Folly" and "Seward's Icebox." But now there was an important southern Alaska city named after the secretary of state who had signed the treaty of purchase with Russia. And she had seen a statue of him, commemorating the act, in Seattle's Volunteer Park.

Seattle! As though drawn by a magnet, Vicki's eyes moved to the address in the heading:

"To:

"JOHN OWERTON GRAVELY, ESQ.
GRAVELY & COMPANY, *Jewelers*
City of Seattle
State of Washington
United States of America"

Somehow, Vicki forced the curious side of her nature to stop there. "You can't read other people's

letters," she scolded herself, "even though this one is so old it must be public domain by now."

A voice from the door of the plane made her jump. "Do you always talk to yourself when you're left alone for a few minutes?" Max was asking. "And don't insult my kitchen utensils. They're not old enough yet to be considered public property."

"I haven't even found your old battered aluminum," Vicki retorted. "Please come here, Max. I need your advice."

He vaulted from the ground to the plane's aisle, and she quickly showed him the letter. "I found it here on the floor between the second and third seats," she told him. "It probably belongs to Mordy, but where can I put it for safekeeping until he returns from his hunting?"

But he wasn't listening. He was peering over her shoulder and calmly reading the upper third of the folded letter out loud:

"'Esteemed Sir:

"'I have failed in my mission. The night before I was to meet Baron Fretzma and turn over to him the Tsar's jewels, I stopped at an inn in Wrangel. Mine host, who I know now, is a retired highway robber, drugged my food. When I awoke in the morning I was alone in the hostel. The jewels which I had hidden in—'"

Max was just about to unfold the letter and continue when Vicki stopped him.

"You can't do that!" she cried, moving out of his reach.

"Why not?" he asked, all innocence. "It reads like a Hollywood script. Crown jewels, highway robbers, wow!"

Vicki laughed in spite of herself. "In the first place, Mr. Lowler," she said, "the letter doesn't belong to you, and in the second, it'll fall apart at the seams if you—"

"What's Scotch tape for?" he demanded. "Hand over that document, Miss Barr. I'm the captain of this ship. It's my responsibility. I have no intention of letting you hand it over to Mordy Mordecaw until I'm darned sure it belongs to him."

"That's true," Vicki said, glad to be relieved of the responsibility. Meekly she let him slip it out of her fingers, and then the letter did fall apart and they saw that it wasn't just one sheet of paper, written on both sides, but four. One of the smaller slips fluttered to the aisle and Max promptly snatched it up.

"'March 5th, 1881,'" he read in the dramatic tones of a radio announcer. "'Jenkins undoubtedly made up this fantastic tale out of whole cloth, and absconded with the jewels himself.' Hum-m. The plot thickens, madam. This little interoffice communication is signed by John Owerton Gravely, who founded Gravely and Company, one of the biggest exporting jewel firms on the West Coast. I happen

to know his great-great-grandson, J. O., the fifth. He paid me a fancy sum to investigate some jade nuggets Eskimos were bringing up in the foothills of the Brooks Range near the Arctic Ocean. But that's neither here nor there. What I want to know is what Johnny's esteemed ancestors' file on the Jenkins case is doing here."

"Oh," Vicki gasped. "Then someone by the name of Jenkins really did abscond with Russian crown jewels back in 1881?"

"Nobody knows whether he absconded or not, for sure," Max told her. "And all I really know about it is from what Johnny said to me half jokingly when he asked me to investigate that jade.

" 'I'd like to get something out of Alaska, Max,' he said. 'It owes us a small fortune. Way back in the latter part of the nineteenth century a courier of ours pulled a fast one with some Russian crown jewels that have never been recovered. Fortunately for us, Alexander II was assassinated shortly after that, and it was somehow settled amicably. But in my granddad's youth the Jenkins case caused quite a furore. Mr. Jenkins died in prison without confessing.' "

Max laughed. "I promised Johnny I'd do the best I could for him, but I found the Kobuk River jade too muddy and murky for gem-stone purposes. And I can't really worry about Gravely and Company's financial problems. Johnny himself is so rich he could buy Alaska at a dollar an acre instead of the

two cents per that we paid Russia for it, and never miss it."

"Now you're exaggerating," Vicki said, laughing. "Nobody has that much money. Anyway, to answer the question you asked a while back, I think it was Mordy who brought this file, as you call it, aboard the plane. Not long after we left Anchorage, I noticed that he was absorbed in something which looked to me like a soiled piece of paper and which he said was a map he had 'drawed' himself."

"Um-m," Max said thoughtfully. "Mordy must have been an urchin of twelve or so when the great Seattle fire ravaged the city in 1889. Kids are usually little scavengers. In the resulting confusion after the fire, Mordy might have snatched the Jenkins file along with some other stuff."

"And," Vicki added, "don't you think that letter would have stimulated any boy's imagination? Why, you said yourself it reads like a Hollywood script."

"True," Max said, "and in a way it *is* a map. It certainly hints that there may be buried treasure somewhere in Alaska, buried by Jenkins before his arrest."

"Then," Vicki went on, "you agree with me that it was Mordy who dropped the file in the Vixen?"

He shook his head. "I won't go that far, Vic. Any of the other passengers might have dropped something during the crash landing. Furthermore, this file might have been lost or stolen during the Seattle

fire. But then again, it might have been stolen last year, or even last week."

He folded the sheets of paper carefully and put them in the pocket of his jacket. "One thing I'm pretty sure of is that whoever brought these aboard the plane has no right to them, since they obviously belong in Johnny Gravely's files. Therefore, I'm going to keep them until I can return them to him."

"You're perfectly right," Vicki said, after thinking for a minute. "So now we know that we have a thief in our midst? If whoever brought that file aboard the Vixen, either on this flight or any other, had any legal right to it, he would have missed it by now and would certainly have reported his loss to you."

"That sums it up very neatly, madam," Max said with a smile. "And it wasn't dropped on any other flight. After every trip I always give my ferry a thorough cleaning."

Vicki smiled back at him. "I won't argue with you, but I still think it was Mordy. Maybe he wasn't bitten by the Klondike bug when he went to Alaska in '97. Maybe it was half a million dollars in crown jewels he was after."

"Could be," Max said easily.

"And maybe he's still on the trail of those lost crown jewels," Vicki went on determinedly. "For he's on the trail of something, Max, that I'm convinced of. And I don't mean a moose, either!"

CHAPTER VI

A Confession

"OF COURSE HE'S ON THE TRAIL OF SOMETHING BE-
sides moose," Max said. "Have you forgotten that he
hopes to find uranium in the rock formation under
the rim of the shelf?"

"So he said," Vicki agreed. "But how is he or anyone else going to climb up that sheer wall to the
rim? If we could, then our troubles would be over.
I noticed, when you were bringing the Vixen down,
that there are jutting rocks from the shelf to the
plateau above the valley. With ropes made out of
the nylon parachutes, I think we could make it to
the top."

Max nodded. "An experienced mountain climber
might," he said, "but there's no sense in considering
that angle, because we haven't a prayer of climbing
to the shelf."

"That's what I mean about Mordy," Vicki said.
"When he hovered above this valley in his helicopter he must have seen that there is no way of getting

to the rim from the bottom. So why did he join our little expedition?"

"I see what you're driving at," Max said thoughtfully. "Jenny never did believe that the old codger was up to piloting a helicopter. It's quite an art, you know, a minimum six-month course, even if you're a veteran pilot." He frowned. "You're implying, I guess, that Mordy is after Russian crown jewels which may be somewhere in this valley?"

"One way to find out," Vicki said, "is to finish reading the Jenkins letter."

And then they heard the sound that was to torment them all for the next few days, the roar of an airplane motor overhead. Vicki stuck her head out of the door, although she knew that the veil of mist would hide the rescue ship from view. Everyone in the clearing was staring up at the veil; Blair Brossard, with a hopeless expression on his face; Jenny, with a philosophical grin; Alec Chapman, white-lipped with frustration.

Suddenly he grabbed up a rifle and fired three shots into the air. Max was out of the Vixen and by his side in a matter of seconds.

"Control yourself, Chapman," Vicki heard him say sternly. "We can't afford to waste ammunition like that."

The engineer's face flamed with anger and shame. "Sorry," he said curtly. "It was a stupid thing to do. But you don't seem to understand. I've got to get out of here."

"So have we all," Jenny said placidly.

"And we will," Max said in an encouraging voice. "Soon as we've had something to eat, Alec, we'll get going on the sailplane. It shouldn't take long to build it. Then, when the wind is blowing from the west, it'll pile up on the east side of the mountain that shields us from the north, creating a powerful tunnel of air. That thermal should carry us up the side of the mountain, over the top, and let us down gently on the other side."

"Then what?" Alec demanded.

"Then we'll be sighted by a rescue plane," Max said easily.

Vicki found the catch on the seat locker then. She gathered up an assortment of pots and pans and joined Jenny in front of the campfire.

"We'll build the glider on the highest point of ground on the valley floor," Max was saying. "Then with a winch and towrope it should be easy to launch her. Once she hits an upward gust of air, she'll soar!"

"I'll help with the building and the launching," Blair said sulkily, "but I'll be darned if I'll ride in a homemade contraption like that."

"Chicken," Alec sneered. "I'll act as pilot."

"None of us three will pilot it," Max said. "We're the strongest members of the party, and our strength will be needed for the launching. Either Hy or Mordy will have to ride in the driver's seat—whichever weighs the least."

Jenny groaned protestingly. "I'll not have my Hy," she began, and then stopped. "Oh, let's not cross any bridges until we come to them." She busied herself making a delicious browned hash out of the cold potatoes and turkey. "We'll have fried stuffing and carrot strips for lunch," she said, "and for dinner we'll have to eat whatever Mordy brings back in the way of game."

"Has he gone off hunting again?" Blair demanded, his blue eyes darting around the clearing. "I thought he was still asleep. He didn't get back last night until almost midnight."

"Oh, what difference does it make?" Jenny asked as she served him a plate of food.

He glared at her. "You were the one who said we shouldn't waste matches and flashlight batteries."

"I know I did," Jenny said placidly. "But I'll bet that old fox can hunt in the dark, like his pack rats." She glared back at him. "And what were you doing at midnight when Mordy returned to camp?"

"He woke me up when he came in," Blair said quickly.

"Then you must be a very light sleeper," Jenny retorted. "When Mordy walks I've noticed that he makes no more noise than a shadow."

Vicki set the coffee on the fire to heat, and then another plane roared over head. It was flying tantalizingly low, and everybody held his breath. Maybe they *could* be seen through that cotton-batting mist. Maybe the smoke from the campfire had somehow

filtered through the veil. Maybe the plane had noticed that it was flying above fog instead of a snow-covered plateau.

In that case, wouldn't it land and wait for the mist to lift, suspecting that the lost Vixen, her passengers and pilot, were somewhere below the blanket?

The last question in her mind Vicki asked out loud. It was Max who answered.

"If the plane is equipped with skis, Vic," he said, "they might land on the plateau. But they can't risk hanging around for very long. The landing gear will freeze to the ground, and you can't always rock it free."

"Oh, dear," she sighed. "Then the rescuers would have to be rescued."

Professor Hyacith appeared then, trotting beside the stream and calling out to Jenny excitedly, "Fossils, my dear, down by the waterfall! As soon as you've finished breakfast you must go down there with me and help take pictures. I'm sure I've ruined this whole role of film."

"I'll help," Blair offered promptly. "On second thought, why don't you rest here at camp and let me do the hunting by camera? I have quite a good reputation as an amateur fotog, you know."

"We didn't know," Alec Chapman put in sarcastically. "And we couldn't care less. All we do know is that you're handy with a knife, and that means you're going to spend every waking minute helping construct the ribs of the sailplane."

"You don't have to be so infernally disagreeable," Blair retorted. "It seems to me that if that old prospector can do just what he likes, day and night, I might be permitted a little freedom now and then."

"The answer to that one," Alec snapped, "is about half a century. A man of Mordecaw's age would be about as helpful in building a sailplane as a babe in arms. Let him spend his time bringing home the bacon. We've got to eat in order to keep up our strength."

"A lot of bacon he brought home last night," Blair sneered. "And I'll bet when he comes back today he won't even have a squirrel in his bag."

"Oh, I don't imagine he's going to spend all his time hunting," Jenny said affably. "He probably left at the crack of dawn with his Geiger counter. He's after uranium, you know."

"Oh, he is, is he?" Blair whirled on the professor's wife. "Didn't you know that his Geiger counter was wrecked during the crash landing?"

"I admire the old boy's attitude," Alec remarked. "Instead of crying over spilled milk, he simply said, when he saw the damage, 'Wal now, there's more than one way of skinnin' a cat.' If our budding novelist would acquire a little philosophy, he might be easier to get along with."

Blair narrowed his eyes. "People who live in glass houses shouldn't throw stones. Since when have you been a charming tentmate? Moaning and thrashing

around in your sleep all night so nobody else could catch even forty winks."

The engineer clenched his fist and took a threatening step toward Blair. "So I talked in my sleep, huh? Just exactly what did I say?"

The tall, broad-shouldered young novelist stood his ground. "Plenty," he snapped. "Enough anyway for me to guess why you're in such a hurry to get out of here." He laughed without humor. "Even rich little boys shouldn't postdate checks to cover gambling debts unless they're sure said checks aren't going to bounce. It amounts to the same thing as stealing!"

Alec stopped him with a slap across his mouth. And then Max stepped quickly in between the two. "That's enough," he said sternly. "Apologize to each other at once, both of you. We can't risk any delay due to broken bones, otherwise I'd let you two silly fighting cocks knock each other out."

Surprisingly enough, Vicki thought, it was the engineer who obeyed first. "Sorry, Brossard," he said contritely. "I lost my temper. You have a perfect right to sock me on the jaw, and you can, the minute the sailplane's ready to soar. Max, here, can tie my hands behind my back then if you like."

Now it was Blair's turn to be contrite. "I deserved that slap," he said sheepishly. "Had no business listening to you talking in your sleep. And what if your check is returned marked insufficient funds? That

could happen to anybody. What's the matter with your old man, anyway? He's got plenty. Is he too stingy to share it with his only son?"

Suddenly Alec Chapman laughed, a bitter laugh. "There's no sense in my living a lie any longer," he said to Max. "I'll feel much better once you all know what a heel I am. The thing is, I don't want Dad to know. He's a great guy and about as stingy as Santa Claus."

"That he is," Jenny said quietly. "Why, McKelvy Chapman is one of the finest men I ever had the pleasure of knowing."

The bitter lines on the engineer's face deepened as he went on miserably, "And I'm about the most worthless son any man could ever have! Dad's always got me out of trouble before, but this time I thought I could cope with the situation myself. Oh, what's the use of beating around the bush? I'll come right out with it. I lost a lot of money gambling and postdated a check to cover it, although I didn't have anywhere near that much in the bank. But you see, when we took off yesterday, I took a chance that we might find this valley and land for an hour or two. During that time I planned to climb up to the plateau. I've done a lot of mountain climbing in my time. Had no idea that the walls would be climb-proof."

"Why do you want to get up on the plateau?" Max asked.

"Because," Alec explained, "there's a valuable

cache of furs up there, and I know exactly where it is."

Vicki swallowed. Fossils, uranium, crown jewels, and now a cache of furs! "What cache of furs are you talking about, Alec?" she asked with a gulp.

He turned from Max to smile at her. "It's all so fantastic you won't believe it, and at first I didn't pay much attention to that note I found in a bottle by the river. But when I saw the professor's ad, I thought that at last Lady Luck was with me. I didn't have enough money to hire a plane of my own and search for a plateau above a hot springs valley, and so—"

Jenny Hyacith, her plump arms akimbo, interrupted. "Begin at the beginning, son," she ordered. "Then you're not a hydraulic engineer?"

He sat down, cross-legged at her feet, and Vicki couldn't help thinking that he was a different person now that he had decided to confess his sins. The petulant frown, the sarcastic sneer were gone, and he looked like a naughty boy who was thoroughly ashamed of himself. "Oh, yes, that part of my yarn is true," he told Jenny. "I was working on a job about ten miles from here as the crow flies, on the Susitna River. Last month I stayed behind at the construction site to see that everything was set for the winter. I was about to check out when I saw a bottle caught in the reeds by the riverbank." He grinned. "Naturally, like the rest of you, I'd been brought up on tales of 'help! help!' notes which shipwrecked sailors

sent adrift from desert islands. So I thought I'd have a look. And, sure enough, inside the sealed bottle was a letter written by a trapper who said he had staggered for miles across frozen wastes only to collapse on the bank of a stream that flows into the Susitna. Realizing that he was dying, he drew a map directing the finder to a cache of valuable furs which he had buried in the snow on a plateau in the Alaska Range not far from a warm springs valley."

Blair Brossard sank down to his knees, wide-eyed with interest. "And you believe what the letter said, don't you? You think there *is* a valuable cache of furs up there? I mean," he stammered embarrassedly, "what I mean is, so many people haven't enough imagination to believe in—well, 'Treasure Island' stuff."

Watching his flushed face, Vicki couldn't help thinking that even after boys grew up they were apt to be carried away with enthusiasm whenever the possibility of buried treasure came up. Actually, the man who had brought the Jenkins file aboard the Vixen yesterday might not have been Mordy after all. It could have been Blair or Alec. But what opportunity had either of them had to rifle Gravely and Company's files?"

"I haven't much imagination," Alec was saying, "and I might have thrown that map away if I hadn't seen the professor's ad one day when I was loafing in between jobs at the family's apartment in Seattle. Dad and Mother had just flown to Honolulu to stay

until after the holidays. I was low on funds, didn't have quite enough to pay my share of even the first flight."

He grinned ruefully at Max. "You made it quite clear on Thursday night that you wouldn't take me along without payment in advance. So the next day I decided to hold a little poker game at the apartment hotel in Dad's penthouse. To make a long story short, I lost my shirt and had to ask the manager to accept a postdated check."

"Humph," Jenny blurted. "So that's how you coped with the situation all on your very own? Why, you silly creature, the manager only accepted that check because of your father's excellent reputation!"

"I know, I know," Alec cried shamefacedly. "But I didn't think about that then. I simply made the check out for a hundred dollars more than I owed, and I didn't worry because I knew from experience that the cashier wouldn't deposit it until after the week end." He shrugged hopelessly. "That was Friday afternoon. Today is Sunday. The check will bounce on Tuesday, and by this time on Wednesday, Dad's sun bathing on the beach at Waikiki will be interrupted by a cable from the hotel manager saying that his son has absconded after virtually stealing almost a thousand dollars."

Vicki suddenly felt sorry for him. She started to say something comforting but Jenny interrupted.

"For pity's sake," she snorted. "How can you say you didn't worry when you postdated that check?

What made you think we'd be lucky enough to find this valley on the very first flight?"

He spread his fingers to stare through them at her in abject misery. "I took a chance on that," he admitted.

Jenny snorted more loudly. "You took a lot of chances. Even if you'd been sure we would find the valley right off, we might not have been able to land. And if we had, we might not have stayed long enough for you to find the furs. And if you had, you might not have been able to raise money on them in time to prevent the hotel's cashier from depositing that check, or to deposit enough money in your own account to cover it. It seems to me," she finished severely, "that gambling has been your trouble all along the line. Maybe a few months in jail will cure you of the habit."

"I don't mind the thought of going to jail," he told her stormily. "I deserve that. But I can't stand having Dad's heart broken."

"What about your mother?" Vicki asked quietly.

"She'll never know," he said bitterly. "Dad will see to that. He's always kept her under glass as though she were a priceless Dresden shepherdess." He jumped up suddenly, his hands clenched tightly to his sides. "I was whistling in the dark last night when I said children should be brought up by nurses and governesses. If I'd had a real mother I wouldn't be in this jam now."

"Now, don't try to shift the blame," Jenny ad-

monished him. "What you did, you did of your own free will."

"I know, I know," he said almost fiercely. "And no jail sentence could equal what I've gone through since that crash landing yesterday."

"Pooh," Jenny said with a sniff. "You haven't yet begun to suffer, and rightly so. What you should concentrate on is a way to keep your father from suffering."

"I think," Vicki began, and then stopped. Jenny was right. Alec had not yet suffered enough for his crime.

"He deserves a little more mental torture," she decided. "I won't say anything to cheer him up until I feel he's been through enough."

She watched him trudge up to the slope with the other two men to start work on the sailplane. "He's a weakling all right," she said to Jenny. "But it must be hard to have the kind of mother who turned you over to nurses and governesses instead of bringing you up herself." She swallowed the lump in her throat. "My own mother—"

"Now, honey, don't start thinking about your family," Jenny said soothingly. "I have a feeling that we'll be out of here before they hear you're missing!"

Vicki wasn't at all sure of that, but there was no sense in worrying. Resolutely she turned her thoughts from home to the Jenkins letter and the Russian crown jewels.

CHAPTER VII

The Courier's Letter

NOT UNTIL AFTER LUNCH DID VICKI HAVE A CHANCE TO talk to Max alone. She was washing the silverware down at the stream when he joined her with the pots and pans.

"Go easy on the soap, ma'am," he said, kneeling beside her. "This little 'yeller bar' isn't going to last forever." Then he lowered his voice. "I finished reading that letter and the other interoffice memos."

"What—?" Vicki began, but he stopped her by dropping the pots and pans with a clatter.

Under cover of the racket, he said quietly, "I'll tell you about it later. The next time I go into the woods with my ax, make up some excuse and follow me." Then he hurried back to work on the glider.

Vicki rinsed the knives and forks and started on the frying pan. Fossils, uranium, crown jewels, and a cache of valuable furs! And who had dropped the correspondence that rightfully belonged in the files of Gravely and Company, Seattle jewelers?

Vicki had felt sure that Mordy Mordecaw was the answer to that question, but now she wasn't so sure. The old prospector had not yet returned to the camp, and still Max had acted as secretively as though whoever had stolen the Jenkins file was close by. Did he suspect Alec?

Could be, she decided, scrubbing the pan with sand. He might have made up the story of a cache of furs in order to hide his real reason for being in the valley. No. She quickly changed her mind. The engineer might have manufactured a tale about finding a note in a sealed bottle, but he wouldn't have lied to the extent of painting himself as virtually a thief. And he *had* seemed convincingly sincere throughout the whole confession.

Then did Max suspect Blair Brossard? Vicki glanced up toward the slope of land where the three men were working on the ribs of the sailplane. Then she saw Max pick up his ax and start out for the woods.

She hastened back to the camp with the clean utensils. Jenny was sorrowfully supervising the simmering of the turkey carcass. "Sad-tasting soup it'll be," she mourned. "No spices, no rice, no nothing to give it a proper flavor."

"I thought I'd take a walk through the woods," Vicki said quickly. "I might be able to find some squawberries for dessert."

Jenny nodded. "And if you bump into our brave hunter tell him I expect caribou steak for dinner."

"If he comes back empty-handed," Vicki said cheerfully, "I'll go fishing in the stream. I saw a sluggish-looking trout this morning."

"You saw *what?*" Jenny demanded.

"A trout," Vicki repeated. "They like clear, icy streams like ours, don't they?"

"They certainly do," Jenny said, starting for their tent. "And sluggish or brisk, I'll have him on the end of my line before the day is over."

Vicki hurried across the clearing and into the wooded area. It was almost dark under the evergreen branches, and silent except for the rustling sounds of birds and little animals. Then she heard the sound of Max's ax and started off in that direction.

"I don't know what these saplings are," he said when she joined him in a small clearing, "but they're the nearest thing to bamboo I ever had the good luck to come across. We'll soar yet, Vic, never fear."

"I do fear, Max," she said soberly. "You're the only one of us who knows how to pilot a glider. And I very much doubt if Hy or Mordy will ever learn what they're supposed to do when it catches a thermal."

"They'll learn," he said grimly.

"I could probably do better than either of them, Max," she argued. "After all, I know a little something about meteorology, and that's the most important factor in flying a sailplane, isn't it?"

He nodded. "Well, we'll see. Maybe Mordy really

can fly a helicopter. If so, he can handle Vixen II in three easy lessons."

"Well," Vicki said decisively, "if he flew over here in a helicopter, which Jenny doubts, could it be that he isn't after something just under the shelf? What was in the rest of the letter, Max?"

For answer he handed her the three sheets of paper and went on chopping down the saplings.

Vicki quickly found the place in the letter where they had left off that morning:

"The jewels which I had hidden in the belt you had made especially for this mission were gone, although I had taken the precaution of wearing the belt when I retired for the night.

"I immediately set off in pursuit of the villain, following the tracks he left in the snow. Then for four hundred miles along the coast, I trailed him, traveling sometimes by post, sometimes by boat, and often as not, on foot.

"I was almost upon his heels, when in apparent panic, he turned north along the west coast of the Susitna River. Nothing daunted, I kept on, and after a day's journey on snowshoes, I stumbled into a small Indian village, called Tulutag. There I learned that the robber had hired a dog sled only an hour ahead of me. I purchased with the last of my funds the fastest team available, following his tracks north and west across the snow. At last I caught sight of him and fired two shots into the air to warn him to stop before I aimed at his person.

"*Almost immediately after that he miraculously disappeared from view. Continuing onward across the mountain plateau I stopped my dogs just in time, for suddenly I found myself not two feet from the edge of a precipice overlooking a valley two thousand feet below. This valley must be fed by hot springs, for there were vegetation and birds in abundance. The peak on which I was standing is also so situated as to protect the floor from the cold wind and snow. But search as I did, I could find no means of descending from any of the heights above.*

"*And then a mist formed above the waterfall that cascades from a shelf halfway up one of the canyon walls, and spread across the valley, blocking out my view. I must conclude that the villain, not so fortunate as I, and looking backward in fright when I fired those shots, was hurled to his death. In my opinion, he and the jewels were buried there for all time.*"

Vicki stopped reading to glance up at Max. "It certainly sounds like our valley, doesn't it? And even if there aren't any crown jewels here, it's comforting to know that, and I quote, 'there were vegetation and birds in abundance' as late as the middle of February."

"There's nothing comforting about that, Vic," he said soberly. "The letter is dated February fifteenth, but Jenkins might have seen the valley sometime during the fall before. In those days it took months to travel distances that now by air take us only a few

hours. Furthermore, under the circumstances, I doubt if Jenkins broke any speed records getting back to civilization where he could find paper, pen, and ink. After all, once he mailed the letter, he knew he would be a fugitive from justice."

"That's true," Vicki agreed, and went on reading.

"And I, since I have failed in my mission, shall bury myself in this forsaken country for the rest of my life, which I hope will be short. I am fully aware that those jewels which Alexander II of Russia purchased from you are valued at half a million dollars. So although I am not truly to blame for their theft, and moreover have served you well, man and boy, for many years, I accept my fate.

"There is no longer a place for me in Gravely & Company.

"You will never see me again, most respected sir, but I remain as always

"Your obedient servant,

"R. L. JENKINS"

Vicki skimmed quickly through the interoffice communication Max had read aloud that morning. The second one was dated June twentieth, the same year, and stated curtly:

"Jenkins arrested. Sticks stubbornly to his story, although we offered not to take the matter to court if he would tell us where he had cached the jewels."

The last memorandum was written in December of the following year.

"Jenkins died in prison, still refusing to sign a con-

fession or to tell us where he had hidden the jewels."

Vicki sighed. "I feel sorry for Jenkins. I think he was innocent."

"I heartily agree with you," Max said. "But don't you see? We can believe his fantastic tale because we're sitting here under that veil of mist created by the warm spring in the valley. You can't blame old man Gravely for refusing even to investigate."

"I suppose not," Vicki said. "There weren't any planes in those days. But it seems to me that his descendants might have made some effort to find a warm springs valley in this locality. Jenkins just might have been speaking the truth, and a half million dollars in crown jewels is nothing to dismiss lightly."

"Whatever happened back in the nineteenth century," Max said, "you can be sure that the matter was not dismissed lightly."

"Oh, I know, Max," Vicki cried. "Don't you see what I'm driving at? Your friend, Johnny Gravely, told you that a nineteenth-century courier stole some jewels from the firm which have never been recovered. If he told you that much, and especially since you said he was half joking at the time, why didn't he go on and mention a fabulous hot springs valley? I think he didn't because he never read this letter."

Max grinned. "I can see what you're driving at all right, hammer and tongs! You're convinced that

Johnny never read this letter because it was stolen long before his time by one Mordy Mordecaw who dropped it in the Vixen yesterday." He picked up his ax. "Johnny," he said, "may never have read that letter simply because he never had any reason to reopen the case."

Suddenly Vicki heard a twig crackle in the densely wooded section between them and camp. She whirled around just in time to catch a glimpse of something green and brown fading into the foliage.

So the old prospector had been slyly listening to their talk of crown jewels! Just in time Vicki stopped herself from blurting out that Mordy had been eavesdropping. Max must never know, for if he did, he would certainly dash right after the old man and accuse him of it. Mordy would promptly deny Vicki's accusation, and since it would be her word against his, the two would from then on be enemies. Matters were bad enough as they were, for Mordy must have heard Max say emphatically that she thought it was he who had stolen the Jenkins file. Even if Mordy was innocent, he couldn't help holding a grudge against her for so strongly suspecting him.

The wisest course, Vicki decided, was to pretend that she didn't know he had been eavesdropping. He, in turn, would have to act as though he didn't know she suspected him. And as long as Max didn't

know that the old prospector held a grudge against her he could have no objection to the plan that was slowly forming in Vicki's mind.

"The first chance I get," she reflected, "I'm going to stalk that old fox when he goes off hunting. It shouldn't take long to find out whether he's looking for uranium or crown jewels."

Aloud she said to Max, "Your friend, Johnny Gravely, may not have had any reason to reopen this case, but you'll never make me believe that he isn't acquainted with every detail of it. That is, unless the file was stolen long before his time. And if these papers were stolen recently, whoever stole them, instead of making copies, is a fool. Besides, who in our party could possibly have had access to Gravely's files?"

"That I don't know," he admitted, "but I suspect everybody except you and me and the Hyaciths. Mordy goes off hunting, but we never hear the sound of a shot. Blair Brossard has none of the earmarks of a budding author. And as for Alec Chapman, I'll believe his yarn when we soar to the top and land on a neat pile of ermine."

"Strangely enough," Vicki said, "I do believe his yarn. But what do you mean by Blair's earmarks or lack of them?"

"Just this," Max said, shouldering his saplings. "He is equipped with about as much imagination as a polar bear. And the writers I know are generally pretty much absorbed in whatever they happen to

be working on at the time. Have you ever heard him mention his plot or one of the characters?"

"No," Vicki said. "But I just took it for granted that he thinks the rest of us are so lacking in imagination that his deathless prose would be wasted on us."

Max led the way back to camp. "Don't be silly," he said over one shoulder. "A real honest-to-goodness author doesn't care whether he's expounding his ideas to a totem pole or a deaf mute. All he wants is a good listener. I played like a good listener last night after we'd zipped ourselves into our sleeping bags. But no go."

"Play like a totem pole next time," Vicki said with a giggle. "But seriously, Max, what bothers me about our young novelist is the bad case of fidgets he gets whenever anyone leaves camp. Why should he worry about the whereabouts of Hy or Mordy? Blair is so selfish my guess is that if anything happened to any one of us, his only comment would be, 'Swell, one less mouth to feed!' "

"He's selfish all right," Max told her. "And lazy. When we started work on the sailplane, he was assigned to the job of cutting down these saplings. He'd be gone for an hour and come back with a mere handful. That's why I suggested that he and I switch jobs. And was he ever burned up! Alec is a slave driver, so Blair can't loaf on the job.

Vicki was silent for a minute, then she said, "Have you ever thought, Max, that maybe Blair wasn't

loafing when he was supposed to be working in the woods? Maybe he's looking for something he, but nobody else, knows is hidden in this valley?"

"My stars," Max groaned. "Fossils, uranium, crown jewels, a cache of furs, and now a mysterious item X. I think I'll quit working on the glider and organize a communal treasure hunt." He chuckled ruefully. "I could use a bit to buy me another air ferry now that my Vixen can't fly even to the top of a wall. I hadn't got around to taking out insurance."

"Oh, Max," Vicki cried sympathetically. "Nobody's even thought to commiserate with you on your loss. We've all been terribly selfish."

"I didn't expect anybody to hold my hand and dry up my tears," he said wryly. "It's just that I'll be flat broke when we get out of here. But I can always get my old job back as a game warden."

"But you must have been pretty sick of that job," Vicki said, "or you wouldn't have quit. If anybody deserves to find treasure here, it's you."

"Oh, I liked the job okay," he said cheerfully. "But it's such a losing battle, it gets you down after a while. Our meat pirates are a pretty ruthless gang. If the slaughter of Alaska's big-game animals isn't stopped soon, they're headed for extinction. The black market," he explained, "is the cause of it all. And the cause of that is the acute meat shortage, which in turn brings us right back to the two most important topics of conversation to an Alaskan— shipping and weather."

"Just who are the meat pirates?" Vicki asked. "Indians? Eskimos?"

"That's right," he said. "Plus coyotes and human coyotes of our own race. The Indians and Eskimos feel they have a perfect right to take from the land of their ancestors whatever they need in the way of skins, bait, and food for themselves and their dogs." The serious expression on his tanned face changed as he chuckled. "Some Eskimos can hardly wait to confess that they killed caribou out of season. Jail to them means a free airplane trip, a vacation with warm blankets on their beds, and all the food they can eat." He grinned hopelessly. "My district covered almost sixty thousand miles of wilderness, so you can see why I think it's a losing fight. Added to which there's a nice little smuggling racket on the Canadian boundary. This gang trades illegally trapped furs for Canadian coyote and wolf skins. These pelts they smuggle back in to Alaska and collect the bounty which we pay for them, thus rooking us coming and going."

"Is there anything you haven't done, Max?" Vicki asked.

"Yes," he said promptly. "I've never been a private eye."

"Well," Vicki said, her blue eyes twinkling. "There's no time like the present. One of your tentmates must have stolen the Jenkins papers from Gravely and Company's files. Your first case will be to find out which one it was!"

CHAPTER VIII

Another Confession

AND THEN VICKI MADE UP HER MIND. "IF ANYONE finds those crown jewels, Max," she said decisively, "it's got to be me! You and the Hyaciths are too busy to search, and we don't trust the other three. If I find them first, half of the huge reward we ought to collect will go to you for a new Vixen; the other half to Hy for his scientific exploration of this valley."

They were at the edge of the woods now, not ten yards from the slope. Instead of working, Blair was staring intently in their direction. Somehow, in spite of her inner excitement, Vicki managed to keep her voice down as she outlined her plan.

"At supper tonight," she told Max, "I'll tell the others that just in case the sailplane won't soar, I'm going to spend all my spare time looking for some way out of here. Then whenever Jenny can spare

me from helping her keep camp, I'll look for the jewels." To herself she added, "And keep an eye on Mordy too."

Max rested the saplings on the ground for a moment. "It won't work," he said, rather tiredly, Vicki thought. "Everyone knows that not even a mountain goat could scale those canyon walls. Whoever dropped that letter will immediately suspect that you found it and are going to try to beat him at his own game. He, or they, will never let you out of his or their sight for one minute."

"I've thought of that," Vicki said calmly. "And the first thing to do is to find out whether it's he or they. If it's just Blair, you can keep him under your thumb working on the glider. The same goes for Alec, although I don't suspect him. If it's just Mordy, he simply can't pretend to be hunting big game at the same time that he accompanies me on a searching expedition. A tenderfoot like me would make so much noise tramping through the woods he wouldn't get a shot at anything with four legs or wings."

"Suppose they're all three in this together?" Max demanded. "We don't really know anything about any of them, remember?"

"That's what I think we should find out this very evening," Vicki said. "It might be just a coincidence that they all answered the professor's ad, one right after another. And don't you agree that if they are

all in it together, one of them would have given some indication of it during the excitement of the crash landing?"

"That's right," Max agreed. "Everyone's attitude then was certainly every man for himself." He took the papers which Vicki handed him then and said thoughtfully, "I don't see how we can ever prove which one of them dropped these."

"We can get a good idea," Vicki said. "The first time we'll all be together since I found them this morning will probably be when Mordy returns for supper. That would be the logical time for you to produce the file and ask who dropped it."

"Right," Max said. "But since the file was obviously stolen, nobody's going to claim it. As you yourself said before, if anyone had a legal right to these papers he would have announced his loss long before this."

"I know," Vicki said. "But if we watch closely, we should be able to tell from the expression on their faces which one stole them. Chagrin, anger, surprise, or fear, somehow or other the man who's after the crown jewels will give himself away."

"Um-m," Max said doubtfully. "And I suppose the expression on my own face mustn't give away the fact that we know the contents?" He grinned. "I'm not much of an actor, so I'll have to concentrate on my part while you do the face-watching."

"Okay," Vicki agreed. "Everyone's attention will be on you, so no one will notice me."

"Swell," Max said, shouldering his saplings. "From now on we're two private eyes representing Gravely and Company although they don't know it."

"I can hardly wait until you explode that bombshell," Vicki said, "but right now I've got some fast berrypicking to do to explain to Jenny why I've been away so long."

"Wait a minute," Max said sternly. "Don't you wander far from camp until we're absolutely sure who the culprit is. After that, I'll never let him out of my sight while you're searching for the jewels. But until then, confine your searching to berries, young lady." He frowned. "I've got to be darned careful not to let our crook even guess you read Jenkins' letter. If he thought for one minute that you know what *he* knows he'd do everything in his power to put you out of the running. Men have committed murder for a lot less than a half million dollars!"

Vicki repressed a little shiver. One man already knew that she had read the letter! Suppose Mordy with his stealthy tread sneaked up behind her while she was picking berries? He could so easily put her out of the running and make it look like an accident.

"I'll be a good little girl," she told Max meekly, but smiling to disguise her inner fears. "I'll remember what happened to Little Red Riding Hood when she wandered off the beaten path."

Max chuckled. "And don't forget it was a woods-

man with a great big ax who saved her life. I've a good mind to issue an order right now that you're not to leave camp unless accompanied by me."

"Oh, don't do that," Vicki wailed. "I've got to find those jewels so we can collect the reward, and—and, something else."

"What do you mean something else?" He glared at her. "You're keeping something from me. I can tell."

Vicki sighed. "It's just that I don't really think you have much faith in that glider, Max. Oh, I know it's going to be a trim little ship, and all that, but you don't really feel that Vixen II will fly even to the top of a porch. Now, do you?"

"That remains to be seen," he said tersely. "I suppose you're implying that instead of wasting our time building a glider we all should be looking for another way out."

"I don't mean that," Vicki said hastily. "I just think that while I'm looking for crown jewels I may as well look for a secret exit. I have a feeling that there is one."

"Feminine intuition," he said, frowning. "Don't let it run away with you."

Vicki laughed and left him then to look for squawberries. But she didn't feel happy; she was worried about too many things. One of them was that Blair, from his stand on the slope, might have been able to see them as they stood there talking for so long at the edge of the woods. If it was he who

had dropped the Jenkins letter, mightn't he guess that she and Max had found it and were conspiring against him?

But in spite of Vicki's worries, dinner that night started out very pleasantly. The three younger men were justifiably proud of the progress they had made in the building of the sailplane. Jenny had caught a rainbow trout and Mordy finally appeared with a plump squirrel which he deftly skinned in a matter of seconds. And the professor was almost incoherent with joy because he had unearthed more mastodon bones down by the waterfall.

Jenny and Mordy did argue good-humoredly over whether they should have squirrel or fish for the main course.

"That animal's got to be put in a pot and allowed to simmer for hours before I'll serve it," Jenny told the old prospector firmly. "Then if you'll hand over some of that sourdough I know you brought aboard the plane in your knapsack, we'll have squirrel stew and dumplings for lunch tomorrow. It'll only take a few minutes to fry this lovely trout."

He bowed gallantly. "Have it your own way, Jen. But I figgered on fixin' up a trap and catchin' a rabbit for the noonday meal tomorrer. Rabbit pie is mighty tasty."

"I'll bake a pie with the squawberries Vicki picked," Jenny told him. "In my opinion, we'll be down to our emergency rations before you catch a

rabbit." She turned to Vicki. "Just what *is* in those three little packages Max donated to each one of us before the take-off at Anchorage?"

"Enough for three square meals per person for one day," Vicki said hesitantly. "But we shouldn't open them until we really have to."

"I'm not going to touch mine until I'm starving," Jenny informed her flatly. "How can you say there's a square meal in a package four inches wide, six inches long, and an inch thick?"

"It's all concentrated," Vicki explained. "Chocolate bars and lump sugar for energy. Potted ham and cheese in one tiny container and canned bacon and eggs in another, for protein. Instant coffee, powdered milk, and lemon powder which can be mixed a teaspoonful at a time in a canteen cupful of water. And each pack contains a vitamin tablet and a stick of chewing gum."

"That's enough," Jenny interrupted in disgust. "Mordy can have my three packs right now to fatten up his rabbit for the slaughter."

The old prospector grinned slyly. "There's hardtack in them little packs too, but I don't aim to lose what few teeth I got left chawin' on 'em. That's how come I brought along some sourdough." He bowed again in Jenny's direction. "What I got in the way of batter, ma'am, is yours. With a few rocks I can fix you up an oven and then we can have meat pies three times a day."

"*If* you bring in the meat," Blair pointed out

sourly. "So far you've only produced one mangy squirrel. I think we should take a vote. I'm quite a good shot. Why don't I do the hunting from now on? This old sourdough can whittle as well as I can."

Max answered his question by reaching into his pocket and bringing out the Jenkins papers. Vicki knew that he had been bracing himself for this moment ever since he had joined the group around the campfire. She herself had shared his nervousness, but felt quite sure that no one else had noticed how silent they both had been.

"We'll take up your point later, Blair," Max was saying coolly. "But now that we are all together for the first time since last night, I want to report that I found these papers on the floor of the plane this morning. Do they belong to any of you? Naturally I haven't read them since they may well be private correspondence."

Vicki's eyes traveled swiftly from one face to another. Alec Chapman did not even glance in Max's direction and kept right on staring moodily into the fire. Mordy's eyes darted from the papers in Max's hand to a point just behind Vicki's left ear, but his face was expressionless. It was Blair Brossard who wheeled on Max angrily.

"You found those papers this morning?" he cried in an outraged tone of voice. "And didn't report it until this evening? That strikes me as gross negligence. It proves that you have no right to continue

in the role of captain. We need someone with a sense of leadership." He appealed to Alec. "Don't you agree?"

"No, I don't," Alec said boredly. "Communal matters must be taken up when all members of the community are present. Mordy departed this morning before anyone was awake and didn't return until a few minutes ago. Producing lost property in his absence when he would not be able to claim it would have been rather negligent, but as it is—"

"Oh, for Pete's sake," Blair interrupted. "That old man didn't drop any papers. Why, I doubt if he can even read."

"Did *you* drop them?" Max asked quietly.

"Of course not," Blair retorted. "I'm not in the habit of dropping important documents."

"Oh, then they *are* important?" Max went on in the same controlled voice.

Blair stood silently facing Max until Vicki said:

"Well, since nobody claims them, Max, you might as well find out what they're all about. Maybe someone dropped them in your plane a long time ago. The only way to discover who did is to look for some identification."

"This is too much," Blair exploded. "Nobody has any right to read that letter." With one swift movement he snatched the papers out of Max's hand and tossed them into the fire. The yellowed old pages turned to ashes almost immediately. Everyone stared at them in a stunned silence.

It was the old prospector who spoke first. "Well, that's that," he said, getting slowly to his feet. "Now that you've elected yourself boss and big-game hunter of this here party, Mr. Writer," he said to Blair, "I guess I'll be movin' along. I don't aim to have a whippersnapper like you runnin' things. And there's plenty of other good places for me to make camp." He reached down for his knapsack and, with it slung over one shoulder, ambled unconcernedly off into the woods.

Alec Chapman suddenly laughed bitterly. "Now you've done it," he said to Blair. "Cut off your nose to spite your face, didn't you?"

"Just exactly what do you mean by that?" Blair demanded, his hands clenched into white-knuckled fists.

"Just this," Alec said blandly. "You may have come along on this jaunt to get material for a book, but ever since you heard there might be uranium around here, you've had itchy fingers. Planned to double-cross the old fox and file your own claim first, didn't you? Was it you who wrecked his Geiger counter? Have you got a nice modern one of your own hidden in the woods?"

Blair's pale eyebrows jerked nervously. "I don't know what you're talking about," he snarled. "I wouldn't even know how to wreck a Geiger counter, and, so far as I am concerned, that old fool can have all the uranium in Alaska!"

Vicki couldn't keep quiet another minute. "I must

say, Blair," she interrupted, "I'm inclined to agree with Alec. Ever since we landed you almost have a fit if anyone wanders off by himself. It looks to me as though you're afraid someone's going to find something before you do." She laughed. "And now you've fixed things so that Mordy is a lone wolf and can search whenever he pleases."

He stood rigidly, his broad back turned toward her so she couldn't see the expression on his face. Suddenly his shoulders slumped, and all the fight went out of him. He sank down on the ground beside the fire and said to Vicki:

"Oh, I admit I've handled things badly and when you've heard my story you'll understand why I didn't dare trust any of you, especially that old sourdough. If he'd found that letter he wouldn't have hesitated to read it. I didn't discover I'd lost it until last night after he'd been gone from camp for several hours. As soon as the others were asleep I sneaked out of our tent and searched the plane. I couldn't do a very thorough job because I had to keep watching for fear Mordy would come back any minute and investigate the light in the plane. When I didn't find it, I jumped to the conclusion that he must have found it first. That type is a regular scavenger—you know, the kind of human jackal that's always on hand whenever there's an accident. He'd steal his best friend's sleeping bag in midwinter if his friend was too incapacitated to protect his possessions. I know those old sourdoughs! And it al-

most drove me mad to think of him, free to find those jewels, while I was forced to spend all my time whittling sticks."

"Jewels?" Jenny asked in surprise. "Jewels in this valley?"

"I'll say there are," he told her. "Half a million dollars' worth of crown jewels which Gravely and Company made up for the Tsar of Russia back in the latter part of the nineteenth century."

"Gravely and Company," Alec interrupted. "So that's where you work, and that's what you meant when you said my mother was one of your best customers! I should say she is. She has her diamonds and emeralds reset almost every year just for the fun of it." He leaned forward, his eyes narrowed. "My guess is that you're on the pay roll as a full-time private detective?"

"That's right," Blair said. "I wouldn't reveal my identity now if that old fox were here. A bird in the hand would be worth tons of uranium ore in that canyon wall to him."

He told them then the story of the Jenkins case ending with: "Nobody connected with my company believed there could be a warm springs valley in the Alaska Range, although we'd all heard of the yarn. Then one day I just happened to see the professor's ad in the paper and promptly brought it to the present Mr. Gravely's attention. He, as promptly, assigned me to the task of joining the expedition incognito. The idea was that, in the role of an author,

I might discover the exact location of the valley without raising any hue and cry. Then, of course, Mr. Gravely would follow up with a large searching party and find the jewels in a matter of hours."

"Well, that explains a lot of things," Jenny broke in sympathetically. "No wonder you've been so touchy ever since we landed. If your boss doesn't get a report from you pretty soon he'll think you found the jewels and absconded with them."

"That's it exactly," Blair said gratefully. "The disappearance of a plane carrying a small sight-seeing party, such as Max here described us in his flight plan, isn't going to make the Seattle headlines. Then think of what a nice spot I'll be in if Mordy finds the jewels and pockets them before we get out of here? Mr. Gravely will never believe that it wasn't I who pocketed them."

"You can put your mind at rest on that score," Max told him. "It's an order as of now that no one boards a rescue plane without first submitting to a thorough search by the rest of us."

"No, no, no," Blair protested. "I cannot allow you all to be subjected to such an indignity for my sake. Besides, I trust you. Just see to it that the old sourdough is searched and I'll be perfectly happy."

"Better include me in that category," Alec said with grim humor. "Since I can't fly up to my cache of furs I might as well line my jacket pockets with diamonds and emeralds."

Blair turned away from Vicki and Max then to

grin at the engineer. "I know your type, Chapman," he said. "You might under duress postdate a check which you planned to make good, but you wouldn't steal a toothpick."

Alec flushed, obviously relieved that his confessed foolhardy act did not brand him as a common thief. "Well, then," he said affably, "it's all settled. We have nothing to worry about. If Mordy should stumble across the crown jewels while searching for moose or uranium, all the better for you. When and if we get out of here, they'll be turned over to you, and at the Seattle end of our journey I imagine you'll collect a fat reward. The chances are, of course, that he won't find them, especially since he's the only one of us who doesn't know they're here."

Vicki bit her lip. Should she confess to Blair that Mordy had been eavesdropping that afternoon when she and Max were discussing the Jenkins case? No, she couldn't, for that would mean admitting that they had read the papers. Such an admission now would make him distrust Max and ruin the happy spirit of co-operation that prevailed around the campfire for the first time since the crash landing. Furthermore, if Max knew that Mordy had listened while she read the Jenkins letter out loud, he would never permit her to leave the camp site, now that the old prospector had deserted. Max would probably jump to the obvious conclusion that Mordy had deserted for the purpose of looking for the jewels unhampered.

But Vicki had slowly but surely come to a different conclusion. Mordy had another reason for deserting, and had seized upon the first flimsy excuse offered him.

She turned to Blair then and said quietly, "I'll help you find the jewels."

Everyone stared at her in surprise. Hastily she explained. "I just thought," she said, hoping she wouldn't put a damper on their high spirits, "that maybe Vixen II won't quite soar to the top of the canyon wall. If it doesn't and cracks up when it drifts down, then there'll be only one thing for us all to do."

"What's that?" Alec demanded, glancing up nervously. Even at that hour of the day, when darkness was near, they could hear the roar of planes somewhere far up above them. "Start a forest fire that might burn away the fog after we've been baked to a crisp?"

"Nothing as drastic as that," Vicki said with a smile. "If we can't fly out, we'll have to climb out. I can't help thinking that if only one of us could get up on that ledge all our troubles would be over. We could signal to the rescue planes from there. If they didn't see us, then an experienced mountain climber like Alec could probably climb up to the plateau where he would be seen."

Blair frowned at her and said surlily, "I don't see what all this wild speculation has to do with your helping me find the jewels."

Vicki flushed. "I just meant that I might stumble across them. I thought that if you all approved I would spend all my spare time from now on examining every inch of the east wall from the valley floor to the shelf for some sign of a passage leading up. Then, if we find that we can't launch the glider, at least that much ground will have been covered."

CHAPTER IX

Vicki Makes Up Her Mind

TO VICKI'S SURPRISE EVERYONE'S REACTION TO THIS
proposal was different.

"You might as well, honey," Jenny said approvingly. "Anything to keep your mind occupied until
the men are ready to try out the glider."

"But my dear," her husband objected mildly as he
peered at her through his gold-rimmed glasses, "we
aren't flies. The musca domestica could easily scale
those canyon walls but not the genus homo."

"She might find some cracks," Alec said. "Then
we could climb using the piton and rope method,
although how we're going to manufacture metal
spikes, without the proper tools, I wouldn't know."

Max frowned at her darkly. "I don't like the idea
of your wandering around all by yourself. We don't
know what you might run into."

"Exactly," Blair said heartily. "She might run into

120

a cave occupied by some wild beast. Therefore, I shall accompany her."

Jenny snorted. "You'll do nothing of the sort. You'll stay up on that slope until the glider is finished. I can shoot as well as any man. I'll go with Vicki."

"Oh, no, my dear," the professor said firmly. "I cannot permit it. You women must stay near the camp at all times."

He peered anxiously over one thin shoulder. "I am not at all concerned by the idea of wild beasts in caves. I have already ascertained that no dangerous animals inhabit this valley. It is the attitude of that peculiar old man that disturbs me. He deliberately deserted us at a crucial moment. Therefore, we must consider him a potential enemy."

"The very fact that Mordy did desert us," Vicki pointed out, "at a time that should be just as crucial to him as it is to us, makes me suspect that there may be a way out of here. And Mordy Mordecaw suspects so too!"

Again everyone stared at her in surprise. "Think back," she answered the question in Max's eyes. "The crash landing—that meant to the rest of us that we were trapped—didn't upset his equilibrium at all. Even when he discovered that his Geiger counter was wrecked, he went merrily on his way. He is busy from dawn to dark and yet all he has produced in the way of game is one little squirrel. Doesn't it seem logical to you that he's searching for a secret exit which he, and he alone knows about?"

Max nodded. "But why the secrecy? What reason can he have for keeping the good news from the rest of us?"

"I can guess," Blair groaned. "He found and read the Jenkins papers before you found them. Now I am ruined! He'll unearth the jewels and escape while we're wasting time on a flimsy glider."

"Calm down," Max said sternly. "The only time he could have come across the papers was last night before you searched or early this morning. And if he *had* found them, you can't convince me that he would have left them there for someone else to pick up and so share the wealth with him."

"Well, I don't know about that," Alec said thoughtfully. "Mordy didn't necessarily have to read Blair's papers in order to guess that jewels are in this valley. An unsolved mystery like the Jenkins case may well have been written up from time to time in the Sunday magazine sections of the Seattle papers. I don't necessarily mean recently, but probably during the latter part of the nineteenth century and the first part of this one. Blair doesn't think our lone wolf can read or write, but of course he can. How do you think a prospector establishes a claim? He writes out a full description of it, places that in something weatherproof, and then builds a stone cairn around it. After that, as soon as possible, he files a formal claim with the government."

Blair nodded. "I lost my temper a while back when I said the old fox couldn't read. But I never

did think he was after uranium. If he'd been hunting that kind of treasure he would have been pretty darn upset when he discovered his Geiger counter was wrecked."

Alec grinned wryly. "From where I sit, we've all been playing right into the old boy's hand. He probably read about the Jenkins case years ago. Then the professor's ad told him that a warm springs valley in this part of the Alaska Range actually did exist, or at least that there was a good chance that it did."

"You've got something there," Max said. "He never flew over here in a helicopter, and just made up that line about it's being only a short flight from Rainy Pass."

"But it *is* only a short flight from Rainy Pass," Vicki pointed out. "He must know more about this valley than we think. There was nothing in the Jenkins file which even hinted that it's exactly where it is." She added quickly, "Was there, Blair?"

Something like suspicion flickered in and out of his eyes, but he said blandly, "Luck, sheer luck, Mordy picking out a spot like Rainy Pass. As Alec just said, we've all been playing right into his hand. As a matter of fact, we all contributed to bringing him here. The first thing you know he'll pick up the jewels, get out, and at the top, add Alec's cache of furs to his booty. Then a rescue plane will pick him up and he'll say he's the sole survivor of a crash landing that demolished the plane and our bones."

Vicki sighed inwardly. They were all overlooking one important point. There was nothing in the Jenkins file which indicated that the valley was near Rainy Pass, nor was there anything in it which indicated that there was any way of getting out. If all Mordy knew about the valley was what he had gleaned from newspaper stories many years ago, then he was no better off than the rest of them. In that case he would never have deserted until after he was sure the glider was a failure.

"No," she said, thinking out loud without realizing it, "I can't help feeling sure that when Mordy came to this valley with us he knew more about it than any of us. During his wanderings he might have met up with a trapper or another prospector who got in and out under his own steam. Whether he joined our party for the purpose of finding the jewels or uranium, or both, isn't important. At least it's not as important as the fact that if he thinks he can get out by himself, then there's a chance that we can too. So don't you all agree that I should start tomorrow trying to find some way for us to get up on the shelf?"

Alec nodded. "You're the logical one. And I personally think it's perfectly safe for you to explore that section of the valley floor. That old fox is probably as crooked as they come, but he's rather gallant with the ladies too. I doubt very much if he'd bop you on the head, Vicki, if you crossed his path."

"Well, I think he would," Max said in such a

fiercely protective voice that Vicki blushed.

"Now, now, son," Jenny said with a loud laugh. "We're not going to let anything happen to our Vicki. I don't think for one minute that the old sourdough knows that there may be crown jewels lying around here. He joined our party for the purpose of finding uranium—uranium he heard was in this valley from some other prospector. I never did believe his story of flying over here in a helicopter. Why, he knows as much about aeronautics as my Hy who thinks a strut is a kind of swaggering walk, and an aileron, half of a church's gable."

"And so they are," the professor said with a puzzled frown. "Just wait till I get my Webster's International—"

Jenny guffawed. "It'll be a long wait, Hy dear. Those volumes are back in our cozy Seattle apartment. And the subject we're discussing right now is ways and means of getting back there as soon as possible."

Everyone laughed except Max who said soberly, "You're forgetting one thing, Jenny. If Mordy answered your share-the-flight ad for the purpose of staking a claim, why wasn't he upset when he discovered that his Geiger counter was broken?"

"Because," she said tartly, "he's smart enough not to overlook the most obvious thing of all. If we don't get out of here, and soon, all the crown jewels and uranium in the world aren't going to do any of us any good." She chuckled. "If Alec's nice warm furs

were down here, instead of up on the plateau, they'd be worth looking for. But since they aren't, I agree with Vicki; the important thing is to concentrate on a way out. You men keep right on working on the sailplane and let her look for an exit just in case."

"Then we're all agreed?" Vicki asked quickly. "I'm to spend my time from now on looking for an exit?"

"I still think two heads are better than one," Blair argued.

Vicki turned to him impatiently. "Honestly, Blair. One would think you didn't trust me! Are you afraid I'm going to find those jewels and say I didn't?"

His face flamed. "It's not that at all. It's just that a man is more likely to discover ways and means than a woman."

"Pooh." Vicki sniffed, and added teasingly, "If you don't stop arguing I'm going to think that *you* are planning to find the jewels and say you didn't."

At that the color drained out of his face as rapidly as it had flamed into it. He looked so angry that Vicki instinctively drew away from him, and hastily apologized.

"Please forgive me, Blair," she said contritely. "I was only joking." As he forced a smile to his taut lips she quickly changed the subject. "You know, Max, I was wondering what Mordy's real reason for deserting us was. His activities were completely unhampered from the very beginning, and all he had to do to keep on being a lone wolf, and at the same time

keep an eye on the rest of us, was occasionally bring home something in the way of meat."

"That's true," Alec said, giving Vicki an admiring glance. "You're a smart gal. Blair's impulsive destruction of those papers couldn't possibly have made him mad enough to pick up his marbles and go home. And neither could Blair's suggestion that they switch assignments. Mordy knew perfectly well we'd all vote that idea down because we need Blair's skill in the construction of the sailplane. Why, *do* you suppose he quit at that moment?"

"I can guess," Jenny put in, grinning. "He didn't like the idea of sharing his sourdough with the rest of us."

Vicki laughed. "I have another guess." She turned to Max. "You know, he slips through the woods and fades into the foliage as though he almost grew there. I was wondering if perhaps he was eavesdropping when you were telling me about your job as an air-borne game warden. Maybe he was once one of your meat pirates and is wanted by the police right now. Have you ever thought what he'd look like with a mustache and a beard?"

"Good grief!" Max cried ruefully. "You've hit the nail on my thumb, Vic! Remember that double-trouble racket I was telling you about?"

She nodded. "The gang that smuggles illegally trapped furs across the Canadian border and swaps them for wolf and coyote skins which they then bring back into Alaska for the bounty the govern-

ment pays for the hides of those predatory animals."
She giggled. "Did I learn my lesson well, sir?"

"You get E for excellent," he said, "and I flunk the
course. The head of that gang was a tall, lean sourdough with a grizzly beard. We never could catch
the slippery old eel, but maybe since I left the service they've at last got something on him."

"We can't be sure, of course," Vicki said. "But
that camouflage he wears made me suspect that at
sometime during his career he didn't want to be
seen from the air. Don't you see? The white outfit
would make him practically invisible in the snow;
and you can't tell him from a tree when he's in that
Brownie suit."

Max nodded. "Those meat pirates are experts at
camouflage. After a slaughter, if they hear a plane
approaching they quickly, and all too convincingly,
arrange the carcasses so that they look alive from
the air."

"Well, it's just an idea," Vicki said. "My theory is
that once he heard you were an ex-flying agent he
made up his mind to desert at the first excuse anyone offered. He *said* he shaved off his beard for fear
icicles would form on it while he was searching for
uranium. But he knew when he started out on that
quest that we were flying to a hot springs valley. I
wondered about him from that moment on."

"You're some little private eye," Max said. "I rec-
ommend that you turn in your stewardess uniform
for a hawkshaw cap and magnifying glass."

"Not me," Vicki told him, smiling. "I've found that in my career I can combine business with my favorite hobby which is scenting out mysteries. But seriously, Max, let's take a vote. If the majority is in favor of it, I'd like to start looking for an exit the first thing in the morning."

"Not on your life," Jenny exploded. "If that old pack rat is wanted by the police—"

"Exactly," her husband broke in. "As long as he is at large Vicki must stay close to camp."

"She certainly should," Blair agreed heartily.

"You all know how I feel about her wandering around by herself," Max added.

Before Alec could give his opinion, Vicki said quickly, "How about a compromise? I'll search, but I won't wander far from where the professor is researching down by the waterfall."

"That's different," Blair said promptly.

"Oh, my, yes," Hy agreed. "No harm can come to her with me about. I may not look very strong, but that old prospector will find out differently if he tries any tricks."

"I guess that suggestion," Jenny told Vicki, "gets our unanimous approval."

Max reluctantly gave in. There was nothing else for him to do. And right after breakfast on Tuesday morning Vicki set off with the professor.

"You know, of course, my dear," he said as he trotted along the bank of the stream, "that when elephants feel that the end is near, they generally go

and lie down near water. Now that I've found those fossils, I feel sure that the area around the waterfall was once the burial ground of prehistoric, elephant-like animals."

"In that case," Vicki said cheerfully, "there can be little doubt that the university will finance a scientific expedition, can there?"

"If only I can be sure that my photographs will turn out well," he said worriedly. "Jenny has convinced me that the rescue plane when it comes will not let me take out any actual specimens. They would be categorized as excess and unnecessary weight."

"I wouldn't worry," Vicki consoled him. "Out of ten rolls of film, you're bound to come up with something convincing."

When they arrived at the waterfall Vicki stared up at the spot where the shelf protruded, now hidden by the veil of mist. Then she turned in the other direction.

She knew that two thousand feet above her a cliff jutted almost rooflike, and protected the floor from the cold wind and snow. And it must have been from the plateau above it that the robber-innkeeper hurtled to his death in the nineteenth century.

Where had his body landed? It was a tantalizing question, for Vicki, if she had only felt sure that the glider would soar, would have liked nothing better than to spend her time looking for the lost crown jewels. But first things must come first, and once

they found a way of getting to the shelf, it probably would be a simple matter from that height to figure out almost the exact spot where the forces of gravity, in conjunction with wind currents, had pulled down man, dogs, and sled. For one thing, the fog must hang thinly there, just as the top layer of a bolt of tulle is almost diaphanous.

If only she could somehow reach that spot! Small as she was, a rescue plane might see her frantic signals. One of them flew overhead right then, and the sound of its motor jarred against Vicki's nerves. The professor was so occupied with his specimens that he had forgotten her existence. Now that she was virtually alone she could give in to her feelings.

Vicki pressed her fingers against her eyelids to keep back the tears. There was no sense in crying, but it was all so hopeless. Soon the search parties would give up. And then what? She had very little faith in the success of the glider project. Even if it could be launched and made to soar, it would take an experienced pilot to guide it above the canyon walls to the lofty plateau. Max was the only one, and his strength was needed for the launching.

Escape by glider seemed hopeless and finding a way to climb the unscalable wall to the shelf equally so. She would have to try, of course, but how much easier everything would be if she knew as much about the valley as Mordy apparently did. He had seemed at home there almost from the minute they landed.

"No bears," he had said confidently, and the very first night had stayed away from camp until midnight.

Another plane flew overhead and Vicki covered her ears with both hands. Resolutely she forced herself not to think about her parents and Ginny, who, at this very minute, might be staring in shocked silence at a telegram from Federal Airlines:

"Regret to inform you that—"

Vicki shook her head to clear it of the mental picture. Mordy, she was sure, wasn't wasting time worrying about what might be going on in the outside world. From the very beginning he had probably been systematically searching for an exit which he and he alone knew existed.

"One good thing about it," Vicki decided, "is that he has undoubtedly done a lot of preliminary searching which I won't have to do all over again. Once I spot him at work, it should be fairly easy to gauge what ground he's already covered."

In another minute she had kicked off her shoes and, with her binoculars slung over her shoulder, was groping her way through the spreading lower branches of a tall blue spruce.

▓▓▓▓▓▓▓▓▓▓▓▓▓▓▓▓▓▓▓▓▓▓▓▓▓▓▓▓

CHAPTER X

Mordy's Story

"THANK GOODNESS MOTHER ALWAYS ENCOURAGED ME to be a tomboy," Vicki reflected as she nimbly climbed up the trunk of the tall, rough-barked tree. When she was dangerously near the tapering top, she braced her feet against a fork, and clinging to the trunk with crossed arms, raised the binoculars to her eyes. It was slow work trying to spot a moving patch of green and brown in the thickly wooded areas at the base of the cliffs, but at last she pivoted into a new position and there he was!

She watched him in amazement for several minutes. Every time the old prospector approached a pile of rocks, he stopped and systematically unpiled them. Then he hurried on to the next heap of stones.

Vicki could have cried with disappointment. "He's crazy," she thought bitterly.

Even if those rocks hid a secret exit, the tunnel they blocked would be too small for any human to

crawl through. Was the old man insane enough to believe that the nineteenth-century jewel thief had survived long enough to cache the jewels under a pile of stones?

Then she remembered something Alec had said the evening before. "How do you think a prospector establishes his claim? He writes out a full description of it, places that in something waterproof, and then builds a stone cairn around it."

Had Mordy flown to the valley sure that there was uranium in its canyon walls? Was he sure because he knew that another prospector had already been there and staked his claim? And had the same prospector told Mordy how he had got in and out of the valley?

It seemed reasonable and it explained a lot of things.

"No wonder the old fox doesn't need a Geiger counter," Vicki reflected. "All he has to do is find his brother-adventurer's claim, destroy it, and substitute one of his own!"

That kind of double cross, Vicki had read, was an everyday event during the Klondike rush. When men were fortunate enough to strike gold they could not resist boasting of their good luck and, as a result, were often murdered by their envious partners. Mordy had grown up during that lawless era, and his code of ethics had probably not changed much with the advent of the Atomic Age.

Then Vicki was struck with another, more cheer-

ing thought. The chances were that the prospector who had told Mordy of his lucky strike in a hidden warm springs valley had probably traveled there on foot, or, as Mordy himself would have put it, by shanks' mare. Any crony of Mordy's must be one of the old Yukoners, few of whom had made or saved enough money to buy or rent a helicopter.

Now, surer than ever that there was a secret exit, Vicki climbed down the tree. She had thought the whole matter through many times and every time she came to the same conclusion. The only way to get in or out of the valley was first to get on the shelf halfway up the east wall.

Mordy's brother sourdough, attracted by the rock formation under the rim, might have tied a long rope to one of the overhanging cornices. Then he could easily have climbed down from the plateau to the shelf. Once there, had he been lucky enough to discover a natural tunnel winding down to the floor?

If so, it seemed likely that when he came out of the tunnel, he found himself under the shelf, or at a spot not far from its shade. "Anyway," Vicki told herself, "that's where I'm going to look—all along that barren strip where nothing much grows because the sun never reaches it."

And the logical place to start, if she was going to keep her promise not to wander far from the professor, was by the waterfall. He had stacked the bones of some prehistoric monster against the

canyon wall on the other side of the stream and was busily photographing them.

"I think you'd get a better effect," Vicki said, smiling, "if you arranged those gruesome objects on the other bank where the light would hit them."

He had been so preoccupied that he blinked at her as though he'd never seen her before. Then he chuckled. "True, true, my dear." He pointed to part of a huge skull and fondly patted the long, mean-looking tusks. "Did you ever see a more beautiful giganteum?"

Vicki laughed. "No, I never did, and thank goodness that one's been dead a long, long time." Then she jumped across the brook to help transport his prize. "When do you suppose this piecemeal monster existed?" she asked as she gingerly picked up a whitened rib.

"At some time between the Tertiary and the Pleistocene period," he said solemnly. "In my opinion huge North American and European mammals intermigrated until the Glacial Epoch. I hold firmly to the belief that where there is now the Bering Strait, there was once a land bridge between Alaska and Siberia. During the Great Ice Age it was flooded. Through fossil evidence we have established that huge camels existed in North America well down through the Quaternary period. Now this mastodon Americanum—"

"Oh, please," Vicki moaned. "Try to speak in words of one syllable, Hy. What I don't know about

geology would fill the Congressional Library."

"But it's all so simple, my dear," he said in a mildly scolding voice. "Now that you are living in Alaska you must inform yourself on the subject of glaciers."

"If I'm forced to live here the rest of my life," Vicki said with a laugh, "I will. I was greatly impressed by the Mendenhall glacier when I first saw it from the air, all blue and green with crystal-clear patches in the sunlight."

He nodded. "To return to my firm contention that the North American Indian migrated from Asia by way of the Bering Strait—"

Vicki stared at him, puzzled and amused. He hadn't been contending anything of the sort, but she listened with interest as he expounded his theory. Finally he came back to the Great Ice Age.

"I imagine," Vicki said thoughtfully, "that this very valley was formed by a glacier."

"Undoubtedly," he agreed. "The frozen debris on the underside of a moving mass of ice acts like a huge sanding machine and polished these walls smooth. That cliff that slopes from the north was left that way after a glacier passed over it, following the direction from which the mass approached. Furthermore," he continued, "in my opinion the original valley here was left hanging after a glacier passed over it. The floor was raised five hundred feet and the stream, as a consequence, became a waterfall."

"How fascinating," Vicki said with interest.

"Then you think that the shelf is all that's left of the preglacier valley floor?"

"I do," he said. "If we were there, instead of here, we could signal to that plane that's passing above us now."

"Do you really think so?" Vicki asked excitedly.

"Why, I'm sure of it," he said. "The warmth is kept in and the cold kept out by the combined effects of the overhanging cliff and the shelf. At the level where the warm air meets the cold, precipitation in the form of a mist takes place. Below that level the air is clear; therefore, I must conclude that above it, the air is clear too."

"If only we could somehow climb up there," Vicki said. "I'm going to look for a tunnel. Do you think there's any chance of finding one?"

"Why, yes," he said encouragingly. "There may well be a subterranean passage through one of the canyon walls. When the tributary valley was left hanging by the glacier, there were almost certainly other outlets than the one that became our waterfall. Although those streams have long since dried up, their beds must still be in existence."

"Well, here I go," Vicki said, hopping across the brook.

But although she started out in a cheerful mood, she ended up so discouraged that she was very near to tears. She carefully examined every inch of the wall beneath the shelf as far up as she could reach standing on tiptoe. It was as smooth as glass.

"Darn that old glacier," she thought crossly. "It certainly left us hanging!" She started back toward the professor, half a mile away. Then a voice behind her made her jump.

"Was you lookin' fer somethin', Vic?"

She turned to look into the shifty eyes of the old prospector. As usual he was staring at a spot just behind her left ear, and for the first time it made her feel uncomfortable. For one thing he wasn't smiling now; and for another, he had his gun in his hand.

Vicki squared her shoulders. The men on the slope of land were too far away to be of any help, but she could see them and that gave her courage.

"Yes, I am looking for something," she said airily. "A way out. Is that what you're looking for too?"

He bared his yellow teeth in an ugly grin. "Now, there ain't no sense in lyin', ma'am. You got a good head on your shoulders. You know as well as I do that we ain't never goin' to get out this here hole."

"I can still try," Vicki said stanchly.

"I wouldn't if I was you." There was a mild threat in his voice, and Vicki felt more uncomfortable than ever.

"Why not?" she demanded with what she hoped was a nonchalant shrug.

"Well, now," he said, playing with the trigger on his gun, "it's this here way. S'pose you was to find somethin' else while you was lookin'. Somethin' that wasn't no concern of yours."

"So what?" Vicki replied. "I'd simply hand it over

to whomever it did concern." She turned away from him as though the discussion had ended. In swift, noiseless strides he came out of the woods a step or two ahead of her, and stood there, blocking her path.

"Beg your pardon, ma'am, but I ain't quite said all I got to say." His voice was downright menacing now, and it flashed through Vicki's mind that even if she did scream, Max couldn't get there quickly enough to be any help. And as for the professor, the best thing to do would be to leave him safely down by the waterfall with his fossils. Perhaps he was as strong as he claimed to be, but Vicki had no confidence in his ability to handle a gun. And she *was* sure that this lean old sourdough was an expert shot.

As though he had been reading her mind, he said quietly, "I don't aim to harm you, ma'am. I jist want to clear up a few little points. F'r'instance, about what belon's to who around here."

Vicki forced herself to smile and say sweetly, "Oh, I see what you mean. You've lost something and want me to give it back to you if I should find it?"

"No," he said, smiling back at her. "It ain't quite like that. What belon's to me in this here valley ain't exactly lost. It jist ain't been found. If you was to find same before me, I want to make sure that you let me know."

"Of course I will," Vicki told him. "Although I don't quite understand."

"Well, now," he said pleasantly. "When you're

lookin' for a cave which might or might not be the entrince to a tunnel, you might come across a pile of rocks. Natcherly you'd take down them rocks, thinkin' they was blockin' the mouth of the cave. And s'pose underneath them rocks you should see a tobaccy can. Then what would you do?"

"I'd open it," Vicki said promptly. "Because, you see, in it might be a message directing the finder to the hidden exit."

He shook his head. "But s'pose I was to tell you that the tobaccy can belon'ed to me, you wouldn't open it, would you, ma'am?"

"Not if you proved to me that it did belong to you." Vicki was sure now that the old sourdough was looking for another prospector's claim. "If it belongs to you," she went on, still smiling, "you can tell me what brand of tobacco was in the can when you put it inside the stone cairn." Too late she realized that she had given him the advantage, for the chances were that he would know what brand of tobacco his crony smoked.

But instead of making a prompt reply, he glowered at her, and Vicki guessed with relief that Mordy was not able to describe the can.

Suddenly the frown left his face and he grinned at her admiringly. "It's jist as I was sayin', you got a good head on your shoulders, and so I'm goin' to lay my cards on the table. I didn't put that can under the rocks, my poor dead pardner did. Joe Lesseyman, by name, may he rest in peace. With his

last breath he says to me, the best friend he ever had, 'Mordy,' he says, 'I'd like to leave you somethin' to remember me by, so listen careful to what I got to say.'

"Chawed up by a bear, Joe was, and hardly able to speak. But I made out that he'd come across uranium in a warm valley somewheres in the Alaska Range. Said it weren't far as the crow flies from Rainy Pass. Said he built him a cairn to warn off other prospectors and put a description of his claim in a tobaccy can inside it. Said he met up with that bear before he could file claim with the govvyment. And the last words he said was:

"'Mordy, that claim is yourn. All you got to do is change my name to yourn and then send a copy of it to the govvyment.'" He grinned broadly. "So now, you know, Vic, what I'm lookin' for and why. I ain't fixin' to make no money out of this here deal. I aim to give all the ore they is in this valley to the govvyment, who needs it bad."

Vicki grinned back at him. "I don't think you'll refuse to accept the reward they'll give you if it's a high-grade deposit."

He looked hurt. "I'm gettin' old, ma'am. Would you begrudge me a few dollars so I can keep from goin' to the poorhouse when the time comes?"

"I don't begrudge you anything that belongs to you," Vicki said cheerfully.

"Well, now, that's real nice of you," he said, holding out a soiled, gnarled hand. "Let's shake on it.

You and me is pardners. If you find the tobaccy can first, I'll see that you git somethin' for your trouble, don't worry."

Vicki shook hands with him gravely. "There's only one thing I don't understand," she said. "A little while ago you told me you were positive that there was no way out of here. And now you're acting as though you were sure of collecting a reward from the government. Did Joe Lesseyman tell you how he got in and out, and have you been keeping it a secret until you could find the claim?"

He focused his eyes on her left ear. "Joe, he died before he could give me the details, ma'am. I don't know nothin' more than what I told you."

"Maybe he landed in a helicopter and got out the same way," Vicki said. "Do you think that was possible?"

He shook his head. "Couldn't say, ma'am."

"But, Mordy," Vicki argued, "if he was your best friend you must know whether he could fly or not, and if he could afford to rent a helicopter."

He shifted and stared at a spot behind her right ear. "I ain't seen Joe for 'bout two years till I was called to his deathbed. I been salmon fishin', ma'am."

Salmon fishing indeed! Vicki thought. He's been hiding out until the hue and cry raised over his illegal activities died down. But she nodded to let him think she had swallowed his tale, hook, line, and sinker.

"I see," she said. "Now I can understand why you didn't dare tell the professor the exact truth when you answered his ad. You don't trust the other men. That's why you said you were going to prospect under the rim for uranium, when all the time you knew it could be reached from the floor. You weren't taking any chances on being double-crossed, were you?"

"No, ma'am," he said promptly.

"And you're absolutely sure, Mordy?" she asked shrewdly, "that we'll find the cairn on the floor? Joe didn't die before he could tell you that much?"

A startled expression flitted across his leathery old face. "Why where else would it be, ma'am?"

"Up on the shelf," Vicki pointed out. Somehow she had to discover whether or not Joe had ever reached the floor of the valley. If he had, then there was a good chance that he had got there by way of a subterranean tunnel from the shelf. And she was pretty sure that Mordy knew that his crony had got in and out by shanks' mare, not by helicopter. Otherwise he would not have deliberately deserted the men who were building a sailplane.

Mordy could not afford to play lone wolf unless he was sure that he could get out by himself. But he wasn't going to share his secret with anyone else until he had to.

He hesitated for so long before answering her question that Vicki repeated it, pointing upward as she said, "Have you ever thought that perhaps Joe

discovered the valley while traveling on snowshoes? Then he might have lowered himself to the shelf with a long rope and found uranium in the rock formation in the upper half of this canyon wall."

"Well, he didn't find it there," Mordy said flatly, then added hastily, "That much he did say before he died, ma'am. Said he built his cairn on the floor of the valley, just as plain as plain, I heard him say that."

"Good," Vicki said. "Then we won't have to worry for fear we're wasting our time leaving no stones unturned down here. Why don't we divide the floor into sections? You work along the west wall while I keep on looking here on the east side. Then I'll search south while you work north under the cliff."

"Smart ideer," he agreed enthusiastically. "And you're goin' to keep this under your hat, Vic, ain't you? I don't trust them others. Chapman, now, he admits he's no good, and that writin' feller, he's slick, he is. Slick as they come."

Vicki nodded quickly, thus promising not to tell either of those two about the claim under the cairn. "Mum's the word," she said. "And now let's not waste any more time. We've got a lot of ground to cover and the sailplane should be ready for the launching some time tomorrow."

"I ain't worryin' about that contraption," he said with a chuckle. "My guess is that we won't be leavin' here fer quite a spell."

"We probably won't," Vicki said. "But how about you?"

But he had already melted into the foliage that edged the barren strip under the shelf. Vicki started back to the waterfall, and by the time she reached it, she had made up her mind. The first thing to do was to eliminate Mordy. For if he won, he might leave the valley before anyone else with two of the prizes and pick up the third when he reached the plateau.

CHAPTER XI

The Stone Cairn

LUNCH WAS SQUIRREL STEW SERVED ON HARDTACK. They all were tired and they ate in a rather moody silence. Then Blair said crossly:

"If you won't let me spend the afternoon hunting, we'll have to use our emergency rations for dinner."

"We'll do nothing of the kind," Jenny informed him briskly. "I'm going to hunt and fish myself from now on." She tossed her paper plate into the fire. "We can't use those things again without danger of ptomaine poisoning. From now on I guess we eat straight from the pots and pans like the Eskimos."

"If you'd let me have the afternoon off," Blair said sulkily, "I could probably find the right kind of wood and whittle out some plates and bowls."

"Oh, for goodness sake," Jenny exploded. "This is getting boring. Why must you always be thinking up excuses for wandering off by yourself?"

He gnawed his lower lip. "I was only trying to be

helpful. And frankly, I, for one, won't eat out of a communal kettle. If any one of us is coming down with something, it'll be an epidemic."

"Shush," Jenny retorted. "Nobody's coming down with anything but you, and thank goodness laziness isn't catching."

"And we don't have to eat out of a communal kettle," Max added. "All four of my pots and pans have lids which can serve as plates for those who are too high and mighty to eat out of a kettle."

He sounded so snappish that Vicki glanced at him in surprise. He looked exhausted; his shoulders slumped, a frown creasing his forehead. She couldn't help wondering if perhaps he had already made up his mind that the sailplane hadn't a chance of soaring tomorrow.

"This is no time," she reflected, "to tell him about Mordy's stone cairn. Max would never let me out of his sight if he suspected, as I suspect, that our lone wolf is not only wanted by the police, but is planning to double-cross Joe Lesseyman, find Blair's jewels, and then climb up to the shelf and make his way to the plateau and back to civilization."

For Vicki had swallowed the hook of the prospector's yarn, but not the line and sinker. There undoubtedly was somewhere near the canyon walls a claim in a tobacco tin inside a stone cairn. But the person who had put it there, she felt sure, had not intended Mordy Mordecaw to substitute his own claim for it.

Joe Lesseyman, if that was his name, hadn't been able to resist boasting of his adventure and good luck. He hadn't even been able to wait, Vicki reasoned, until he had filed a formal claim with the government. And now for some reason he was being prevented from protecting his interests.

Vicki didn't like to think what that reason might be. Had Mordy lured him to a lonely cabin and left him there, bound hand and foot? In that case, Mordy would be guilty of unpremeditated murder if they all didn't get out soon.

Later, when she and Jenny were washing the silverware and the stew pot down by the stream, Vicki repeated the prospector's yarn. When she had finished she said:

"It's going to be a race from now on between that old fox and the rest of us. I don't think we ought to drag Hy into this, and the younger men are needed for the building of the sailplane. Therefore, it's up to you and me."

Jenny nodded soberly. "If we can catch him in the act of destroying that claim, we can keep him under guard from then on. Those three men up on the slope aren't going to pay any heed when he insists that it was Joe Whatyoumaycallum's dying wish that Mordy inherit the reward."

"Nobody in his right mind would believe that yarn without something in writing or witnesses," Vicki agreed. "If Joe Lesseyman died intestate and without heirs, the uranium in this valley belongs

to the United States Government, doesn't it?"

"I should think so!" Jenny said emphatically. "But my guess is that Joe is alive, although obviously not able to kick. The first thing we've got to do, is separate the old fox from his rifle, and that I shall do this very afternoon."

Vicki couldn't help laughing. "How on earth are you going to do it?"

"Simple," Jenny said smugly. "I'm going hunting myself this afternoon, and I'll keep to the woods along the west wall. It takes two hands to unpile a heap of stones, so while he's thus busily engaged, I'll sneak out from behind a tree, snitch his gun, and sneak back."

Vicki stared at the plump woman in amazement. "Do you think you can get away without his hearing you?"

"Of course," Jenny said with a toss of her head. "I can walk through the woods without crackling a piece of moss. My father taught me when I was a little girl how to stalk moose and it's something you never forget, like bicycling."

"My goodness," Vicki cried. "You're like Max. Is there anything you haven't done?"

"Not much," Jenny said with a grin. "I've never stalked a human before, but there's no time like the present. And after I get his gun, I'll keep on stalking until I catch him red-handed."

"Then," Vicki pointed out, "you'll need a witness. Otherwise, it'll be his word against yours."

"Oh, my goodness," Jenny groaned. "I never thought of that. We can't spare the younger men from the sailplane, and you've got to spend all your time looking for all the things you're looking for, so my witness will have to be Hy."

Vicki shook her head. "No, Mordy might be able to convince Blair and Alec that your husband was simply backing up your fantastic tale, and that he had been framed. Hy is so absent-minded he wouldn't be a good witness, anyway, if the matter comes up in court. Max has got to be there when Mordy tries to destroy that claim."

Jenny only groaned more loudly. "You can't get him away from that sailplane, Vicki Barr, unless you tell him the whole story. Then he'll want to do the stalking and ruin my fun. And if I don't have some fun soon, I'll blow up. Honest to goodness! With nothing but two tents and four pots and pans plus a few knives and forks to keep clean, I'll go berserk. I'm used to fussing and cooking and baking from dawn to dark. Don't you dare bring Max into this."

"I won't," Vicki promised, "until the very end. And I think we can arrange to have him among those present at the right time, because, you see, I'm pretty sure I know where that stone cairn is!"

"You are?" Jenny's black eyes were round with amazement. "Where is it?"

"Down by the waterfall," Vicki said. "This morning I helped Hy arrange some gruesome old bones in a lifelike attitude so he could photograph them.

That was right after I'd seen Mordy unpiling stones along the west wall and was beginning to suspect that he was trying to find another prospector's claim. On the west side of the stream there's a pyramid of rocks which looks as though it had been built by a man, not by nature. So I draped what was left of the mastodon's ribs over it and we built up the skeleton from there."

She giggled. "I honestly didn't think much about it at the time, Jenny, because Hy was telling me about glaciers and I had to concentrate like anything to understand his language. But after I talked with Mordy, I felt pretty sure that he *was* planning to double-cross another prospector, and so—"

Vicki suddenly found herself enfolded in Jenny's arms. "You out-camouflaged that old camouflager, honey," she crooned delightedly. "Even if he snoops around down there tonight I'll eat my hat if he's smart enough to figure out that Joe Whatyoumaycallum's claim is hidden under a pile of rocks which is under a pile of bones."

Vicki nodded. "I think ever since we landed Mordy has been systematically searching, working from south to north along the west wall. At least that's the way it looked to me when I saw him from the top of the blue spruce this morning. If he'd started from the north end and worked along the east wall, he long ago would have seen that pyramid down by the waterfall."

"That's right," Jenny agreed. "And furthermore,

he's been delayed because he apparently stops every now and then to spy on the rest of us and make sure one of us won't find the cairn first. He must have seen you searching under the shelf this morning, Vicki, and hotfooted it right over there." She chuckled. "But now that he thinks of you as little helper, he won't waste any more time spying. If you can give me some idea of where along the west wall you think he'll be working this afternoon, I'll go right off and get his gun."

Vicki thought for a minute. "My guess is that he would be a half a mile from the waterfall as the crow flies."

"Good," Jenny said. "Then it shouldn't take me much longer to stalk him and swipe his gun than it should take you to get to the bottom of the bones and rock. If you have accomplished your mission successfully, hang the hood of your red parka from a branch of the blue spruce as a signal to me that all's well. Stay up in the tree with your binoculars leveled on the camp. If you see me return with two guns, you'll know I accomplished mine successfully. Then you can go off and bring Mordy back to the trap."

"Fine so far," Vicki said approvingly. "But what will he do when he discovers his gun is gone? Trail you back to camp and demand the return of it?"

"He's too sly for that," Jenny said emphatically. "He'll plan on raiding the men's tent tonight when we're all asleep."

"That's what I think," Vicki said. "Now the only hitch is that while I'm telling Mordy I think I've found his cairn, how are you going to lure Max away from the sailplane's wings?"

"That," Jenny said with a chuckle, "will be the easiest chore of all. I'll simply tell him that you and I arranged that if you ever needed help you'd hang the hood of your parka on a branch of the blue spruce. When Max sees that spot of red down by the waterfall, he'll be off like a rocket. Once we get there, I'll yank him behind the spruce and keep his blood pressure down by telling him the whole story. You should show up with that old pack rat before Max insists upon blundering off on your trail."

"Oh, I don't think he'll worry about me once he knows Mordy hasn't a gun," Vicki said. "You could tell him about our trap on the way down to the waterfall."

"Not with him running at top speed to rescue his favorite maiden in distress," Jenny said, laughing. "And I don't dare say much in front of the others up on the slope. That Blair would insist on coming along too, and sure as anything, we'd lose him en route."

"I know what you mean," Vicki said thoughtfully. "He's awfully, awfully anxious to find those jewels himself, isn't he? Do you suppose he doesn't trust me?"

"That one doesn't trust anybody," Jenny said with a sniff. "Not even himself, and there I agree with

him. Half a million dollars in crown jewels would be mighty tempting to any young man, no matter how big a reward he may be going to collect at the Seattle end."

"I'm glad you feel that way," Vicki said. "Because I've just about made up my mind that if I do find the jewels, I'll turn them over to Max and suggest that he by-pass Blair and give them to Mr. Gravely himself. Blair can still collect the reward, although I think he ought to share it with Hy and Max. If it hadn't been for Hy this valley might never have been found just when the veil was lifted. And Max certainly deserves something to compensate for the loss of his Vixen."

"He certainly does," Jenny agreed as they strolled back to the camp. "But Blair isn't one to share anything with anybody. Oh, I know he's here as the company's representative, and, as such, the jewels, if and when they're found, should be turned over to him. But just the same, I'm glad you're not going to place temptation in that young man's path. In fact, if I were you, I wouldn't even tell Max if you should happen to stumble across them. You'd have a hard time convincing him that he should by-pass Blair."

"I know," Vicki said, frowning. "Max is in no mood to listen to our suspicions of Blair, which, I suppose when you get right down to it, are based on nothing but feminine intuition."

"If you should ask me," Jenny said, "my feminine intuition would tell you that Max is depressed be-

cause he knows that unless the wind's right, his contraption won't fly more than a few feet from the ground. I think they should abandon that project and help you find a way out of here. You've convinced me that there is one."

"I'm almost sure there is," Vicki said, "but unless I find it before the rescue planes give up, it won't do us any good. Max says that none of the regular air routes pass anywhere near the plateau, and the chances of a bush pilot flying over it before winter seeps down here are about one in a million."

Jenny shivered. "And that time isn't too far off. The squirrels are as busy as can be gathering nuts. They'll be hibernating soon, and so far as I can see they're the only edible animals in this valley. When the birds are gone and the stream freezes solid, the only way we'll be able to get meat is by fishing through a hole in the ice. And we won't get much that way because they're not so many fish in that stream that they form a bridge across it. Your one lazy trout is the only one that's nibbled on my hook, although I worked at it most of the morning."

"Well," Vicki said, more cheerfully than she felt, "we can always make our emergency rations last three days if we have to. Right now let's concentrate on some way to keep Hy from going back to his mastodon down at the waterfall. I don't think he should be around when we spring the trap, do you?"

"I certainly don't," Jenny agreed heartily. "He'd be sure to ruin everything. I tell you what I'll do.

I'll sit him right down by the stream here and tell him he can't move until he catches something to eat." She chuckled. "He'll promptly fall asleep, as he always does when he goes fishing, so even if he does have fool's luck and gets a nibble, he won't know it."

"Well, then," Vicki said, "that takes care of everything."

She ducked into their tent and unzipped the hood from the rest of her red parka. Then she and Jenny said solemn good-byes and set off in different directions.

When Vicki arrived at the waterfall she was out of breath as much from excitement as from hurrying. It took a long time to dismantle the mastodon and neatly stack the bones on the ground. No matter what happened she was determined not to harm any of the professor's treasures. Then at last she was tearing down the pyramid with haste-clumsy fingers. When she had lifted off the top stones she reached inside, groping. Sure enough, her fingers soon closed over a tin can!

But still Vicki couldn't believe that she had found Joe Lesseyman's claim until she had read the penciled note she found in the can, and saw his signature and address at the bottom of it. Then she carefully copied every word in the claim on another scrap of paper and substituted it for the original. Things might go wrong. She was not going to let Mordy spring the trap and get away with the bait.

Now to put everything back in place so that he wouldn't guess that she had investigated the inside of the cairn.

In a few minutes more, Vicki was climbing up the blue spruce to the same perch she had occupied that morning. As she neared the top, the branches grew shorter so it was easy to reach out and drape her hood over the end of one of them. Then she peered through her binoculars at the camp.

The three younger men were putting the finishing touches to the sailplane, and the professor was nodding beside the stream. There was no sign of Jenny.

Vicki stared until her eyes ached. It seemed like hours until at last the plump woman emerged from the woods, triumphantly carrying two rifles.

Vicki climbed down so quickly she almost fell the last few feet. Without waiting to catch her breath she hopped across the stream and darted into the woods. Then she pushed her way through the trees, shouting, "Mordy, Mordy!" every few minutes.

Finally she heard an answering hoot and yelled, "Mordy, I think I found your cairn!"

He came swiftly toward her and Vicki knew from the wicked gleam in his eyes that he was inwardly seething because he had been robbed of his rifle. Suppose he suspected her of the theft! It was almost dark under the leafy evergreens, and the camp was very far away. For a moment Vicki was tempted to turn and run, and then he grabbed her arm.

"Don't stand there starin' like a dead fish," he yelled, half dragging her along. "If you found a cairn lead me to it, and no loiterin' on the way."

Vicki pulled herself free, and was thankful to realize that the professor was right. The old sourdough was lean and wiry, but he actually had very little strength in his arms. "How can I lead you to it if you insist upon dragging me in the opposite direction?" she demanded tartly.

Instantly his attitude changed. "Beg your pardon, ma'am," he said humbly. "I got so het up when you yelled at me I guess I sort of fergot myself. Where do we go?"

"Down by the waterfall," Vicki said, starting ahead of him. She didn't like the idea of turning her back to him, but there wasn't room enough between the trees for them to walk side by side. "I'm not sure it's the right pile of rocks," she said, hurrying as fast as she could to get out of the woods. "But it's sort of a pyramid and looks like a man had built it."

"So you didn't look inside for a tobaccy can?" he said. "Jist raced right off to find me, eh? And how did you know where to look?"

"Why, Mordy," she cried innocently. "Only this morning we decided that you would search the west wall, remember?"

"So we did," he answered in a mollified tone of voice. Suddenly he became suspicious again. "Say now," he said, "I had a good look around down by

that waterfall the other day and I didn't see no pyramid."

"And I can guess why," Vicki said quickly. "The professor probably had it covered with whatever specimens he was photographing at the moment."

"Nope," he told her when they came out of the wooded area and he could now see the cairn for himself. "He wasn't photographin' when I was watchin', but he was standing knee-deep in old bones. Guess they blocked my view."

He skipped nimbly by her and across the brook. Then with a delighted chuckle he pushed off the top stones and reached inside. Vicki didn't dare look in the vicinity of the blue spruce where she hoped two pairs of eyes were watching.

In another second Mordy had Joe's claim in his hand and was holding it against his nose as he mouthed out each word. If he's that nearsighted, Vicki decided, he probably wears glasses when he wears a beard and isn't wanted by the police. And then, as though to prove her suspicions, he squatted on the ground and produced spectacles, a stub of a pencil and a scrap of paper from his jacket pocket.

He seemed to have forgotten her existence as he peered through the glasses at the claim and laboriously copied down the description, muttering and mumbling to himself all the while. Vicki thought he would never finish spelling out each word.

But at last she could see that he was signing his

own name to the fraudulent claim with a triumphant flourish. And then Max stepped out from behind the blue spruce.

"Just what do you think you're doing—?" he began and suddenly stopped, gaping with surprise. "Why, Mose Nelson," he finished with a delighted grin, "I never would have recognized you if you hadn't forgotten to shave and donned your specs."

The old prospector scrambled to his feet, his clenched fists crumpling both claims. "I ain't no Mose Nelson," he whined. "You ain't got nothin' on me."

"Not much," Max said. "I've been shown your photograph too often to forget that you're suspected of dealing in the black market, smuggling, and shooting and trapping out of season."

"You can't prove nothin'," the old man shouted defiantly.

"No, I can't, here and now," Max admitted sternly. "But I'll bet when we get to Juneau we'll find a lot of other people who can. Hand over those papers, Nelson. I guess I just stopped you in time to keep you from adding filing a fraudulent claim to your list of crimes."

With one deft flick of his gnarled hands, the sourdough tossed the two scraps into the waterfall. "Fish 'em out, son," he said cheerfully. "They'll be so water-soaked by that time that you and nobody else won't be able to read a word."

Vicki spoke up then. "It doesn't matter," she told Max. "I have the original claim in my pocket. He threw away two worthless copies."

"You idjit you!" Mordy snarled. "Why'n't you keep your mouth shet? I was goin' to split fifty-fifty with you."

At that Jenny appeared with a cocked rifle under her arm. "Well, well, Mordy Mose Nelson," she chortled. "So nice of you to confess before witnesses that you planned to destroy Joe Whatyoumaycallum's claim!"

At the sight of the gun he began to whine again. "I was only doin' what a dyin' pal ast me to do."

"Whether he's dead or alive remains to be seen," Jenny said, adding briskly, "Now get along back to camp. It's a nuisance, but I guess we'll have to take turns keeping an eye on you after this."

"It *is* a nuisance," Max agreed, "but it won't be for long I hope. If the wind is right tomorrow, the sailplane will be ready to soar."

"Then," Vicki said decisively, "I'd better spend the rest of the day brushing up on my aeronautics. Because, Max Lowler, I'm the one who's going to ride in it."

CHAPTER XII

Behind the Waterfall

IT TOOK TWO HOURS OF STUBBORN ARGUING FOR VICKI to make Max understand that Professor Hyacith was completely incapable of soaring.

Max glared at her crossly. "What makes you think you'll be any better at the controls?"

"Well," Vicki said wearily, "before I could be graduated from Stewardess School, I had to acquire a little knowledge of what the pilot's job is. And since then, I've been studying every spare moment I've had, because some day I plan to take flying lessons and get a pilot's license."

"Some day," he said, "is not tomorrow."

Vicki held up one small hand to silence him. "Furthermore, Jean Cox, who was in my class, owns and pilots a Piper Cub. When she was only fourteen her parents gave their consent and she got a student glider permit. That same year she broke the state record for distance and time in the air. Jean has told

me so many of her exciting experiences while soaring that I feel sure, after a few instructions, I won't have any trouble keeping Vixen II up in the air."

"There's no harm in letting her try," Blair pointed out.

"And I agree with her," Alec added, "that letting the professor have a crack at it will only end in a crack-up. Then all the work we've done will have been wasted."

"I'm terribly sorry I'm so stupid when it comes to anything mechanical," Hy said, suddenly waking up from his nap by the stream. "But perhaps I could learn."

"Perhaps you could," Jenny said tartly, "but it would take months. "No, Max," she went on unhappily, "Vicki is the one. I'm too heavy, but my weight will come in handy when I lean on the towrope. Why don't you let her demonstrate how much she knows right now?"

"All right," Max said, reluctantly leading the way up to the slope.

The little homemade craft looked frail and discouraged, her nose and one wing resting on the ground, the other pointing skyward. Vicki crawled into the cockpit.

"I know one thing," she told Max. "Once I'm adrift from the towrope, I should keep the nose slightly down, because I must slide slowly down the same hill of air that will be carrying me up. And," she added shrewdly, "there's really nothing to worry

about. If the wind should desert me, I'll simply spiral down and land as gently as a leaf."

"That's true," he admitted after thinking it over. "People almost never get hurt in glider crash landings, although the craft is often wrecked."

Vicki touched the stick. "If I move it to the left, the right wing comes up, and if I push on the left pedal, the sailplane goes left. Right?"

"Right," Max said. He hesitated a moment and then gave in. "Okay, I guess you can manage with some more instructions. I don't like any part of it, but," he went on in a low grumble, "the chances are we won't even be able to launch the darn thing. Jenny will have to stand guard over Mordy to keep him from making a break for the woods, so—"

"I won't do any such thing," Jenny boomed. "I'll hobble the old fox so that all he'll be able to do is roll like a hoop. And if he does that, he'll land in the stream which will do both his body and soul good."

"Ah, you don't have to tie me up," Mordy said with a grin. "I ain't goin' to run off nowhere. I aim to stay right here and see the fun. If that contraption leaves the ground I'll eat my fur boots."

"Keep a civil tongue in your head," Jenny admonished him, "or that's all you'll get to eat from now on."

Everyone, even the old prospector, laughed. So at last it was decided, and early the next morning the glider was launched with Vicki at the controls.

The first thing that struck her with a thrill was

that she was rising above the ground and yet there was no sound of a powerful motor. Suddenly she felt a lift and knew she had hit a thermal. Quickly, and a little nervously, she pulled the release knob that would set her adrift from the towrope. Now she was on her own, soaring with the rising upcurrent of air. She felt like a bird with slim, tapering wings; she and Vixen II were one and the same! Up, up they went, into the first thin layer of the mist. How close were they to the shelf? Should she push on the left pedal in order to avoid crashing into it? No, for when she rose higher, she might crash into the overhanging cliff—the cliff that had proved the nemesis of the nineteenth-century jewel thief. Max had said to stick to the thermal, but—

For a split second Vicki took her eyes off the controls long enough to glance up and then, sickeningly, down. Above her loomed the awesome, shadowy outline of the mountain peak. It was agony not to push on the right pedal in order to avoid being drawn up to it like a nail to a magnet. But somewhere in the cream-sauce mist, not too far on her right, jutted the shelf. It was like riding straight up in an elevator to certain death.

Just as the mist cleared sufficiently to reveal to Vicki that the sailplane was at the level of the shelf, a powerful steady current of air caught her frail craft and blew it down-valley, away from the waterfall. As she described it afterward to Max, it was just as though someone suddenly had turned on a

giant electric fan. In the moments that followed, Vicki was too busy to attach any special significance to this powerful air drift which carried her glider and the layer of mist rapidly before it. It took all of her strength and instinct to fight the controls, until at last she was able to steer her craft away from the looming canyon and down into quieter air.

And then she began to spiral, slowly, slowly, down, down.

The craft settled as gently as a bird in the clearing midway between camp and the waterfall and directly opposite a pine grove in the thickly wooded section. Vicki unbuckled her safety belt and climbed out. What had gone wrong? She had done everything Max had told her to do.

He was running in her direction, and although her knees were shaking she hurried to meet him halfway.

"You're okay?" he called from a distance.

Vicki shook her head up and down. "What did I do wrong?"

"It wasn't your fault," he said. "The draft petered out too soon. You were dropping a foot for every five you were rising."

"It didn't seem like that to me," Vicki said wryly, remembering how she had been torn between pushing on the right or the left pedal.

"Well, anyway," Max said, "that's that. We can't launch her from here, so we'll have to dismantle her and carry her back to the slope piecemeal. That'll

take all day and then we'll have to wait until we're sure of a tunnel of air that'll carry you up and over the mountain." His shoulders slumped disconsolately. "Frankly, Vic, I'm not as optimistic as I was in the beginning. If we could see the cloud formations that mark the tops of the thermals, we could get out of here. Or, if we had an up-to-date craft, with a glide ratio of at least twenty to one, we could make it."

He kicked a pebble into the brook. "But with that makeshift crate, plus a blanket of mist between us and the sky, I just don't know."

"Oh, let's not give up so easily," Vicki said, and then stopped.

"Max," she cried, "perhaps this flight wasn't a complete dud, after all. You probably couldn't see from down here on the valley floor, but when we got up to the level of the shelf, a steady current of air struck us. It must have been of a thirty-mile-per-hour velocity. It almost flopped the glider on her back. I managed to blunder out of it and get down to quieter air, but now that I think of it, I'm willing to bet that the current of air is there constantly—has something to do with the mountain peak, the valley, and the warm air above the springs."

"Very interesting, Vicki," replied Max with a puzzled frown, "but so what?"

"Well, it means that anything that came hurtling off the plateau would have something besides gravity to contend with," she replied.

A chill wind suddenly rushed down through the veil of mist, bringing with it flurries of snow which melted into the spray of the waterfall. Vicki shivered although she was still wearing the warm clothing which she had donned for the flight up and over the mountain: the red, fleece-lined parka and fur-lined boots. In case the glider should come down on a spot inaccessible by plane, Max had taught her how to signal with her arms the word "helicopter."

Now Vicki couldn't help feeling grateful that Vixen II had come to roost back in the valley. No planes would be flying overhead if there was a snowstorm; no one would have seen her flailing red sleeves. Max had filled her pockets with matches, flashlights, and emergency rations, but with snow falling thickly could she have set fire to the glider? Would anyone have seen the smoke? Would anyone have seen her frantic signals by flashlight at night?

As though reading her thoughts, Max was saying in a strange, throaty voice, "That settles it. You do no more soaring, Victoria Barr."

Vicki didn't say anything for a minute. She was still frightened at the thought of what might have happened to her. And she was still thinking about a dog sled and its driver caught in a powerful current of air. But what was the alternative? Soon the rescue planes would give up the search. In a few weeks it would be as cold in the valley as it was on the plateau.

She squared her shoulders resolutely. "We don't

know for sure that it's snowing up above, Max," she said in what she hoped was a brave voice. "A gust of wind could be blowing snow down from the peak. Let's try again. Maybe we can launch her from here."

"Don't be ridiculous," he said sternly. "Even if we could, I wouldn't let you ride in her."

Vicki glanced upward to where she now knew the overhanging cliff loomed. Max was right. They couldn't launch the glider from here, or for that matter, from any other spot in the valley except the slope of land. And snow was now mingling thickly with the mist above the waterfall.

Alec and Blair joined them then. "I guess there's a raging blizzard overhead," Alec said. "Lucky for you, Vic, that you didn't make it up and out of the valley. No rescue planes will fly over today."

"Or tomorrow," Blair said. He slapped the glider's nose peevishly. "After all that work, the darn thing isn't as good as a kid's kite."

"A kite," Alec suddenly shouted. "That's the thing! We can build one in a few hours. With all the turbulence around here, it'll soar up and out."

"What fun," Blair said sarcastically. "What a jolly good time for all. My!" He wheeled away from them. "You two can pass the time playing around with sourdough paste and splinters, but I'm through!" He jumped across the brook and disappeared in the woods.

"Quitter!" Alec shouted after him, and said in a

quieter voice to Max, "If he'd let me finish I would have explained that we could attach a map to the tail of the kite, showing our exact location, and indicating that we can only be rescued by helicopter."

"A swell idea," Vicki agreed, thinking: Anything to keep up their spirits. "We could wrap the map in one of the waterproof matchbox containers. What do you think, Max?"

"I've stopped thinking," he said forlornly. "My brain hasn't functioned since I realized that you might have soared right up and into a blizzard. And how could a kite fight that air current, if a much heavier glider couldn't?"

"It was certainly not an ill wind that dropped me gently down to the floor," Vicki said with a smile. "So let's be thankful for something. Why don't you two build a kite? It's worth a try, and there's no sense in trying to dismantle and move the glider until Blair gets over his sulks and comes back."

Professor and Mrs. Hyacith, one on each side of the old prospector, joined the others.

"You'll do no such thing," Jenny boomed. "A kite isn't going to get us out of here, and neither is that flimsy glider. I know enough about aeronautics to realize after one trial flight that it just hasn't got what it takes."

"You're absolutely right, Jenny," Max said forlornly. "A plane could tow her to an altitude of a thousand feet, and then she might keep soaring. But man power isn't enough."

"And so," Jenny went on with a nod, "we won't waste any more time on her. What we'll do from now on is divide the valley into sections and search for a hidden exit." She pointed her rifle at Mordy. "This old weasel knows where it is, but he won't tell."

"Oh, he won't, huh?" Alec took a menacing step toward the prospector. "Just leave him alone with me for a few minutes. I'll make him talk."

"None of that stuff, Alec," Max said quickly. In a quiet voice he asked Mordy, "Why won't you tell us where to find the way out? It's not going to do you any good to keep it a secret."

The old man snorted. "It ain't goin' to do me no good to let you in on it." In a cunning whine he added: "Now, if you was to promise to fergit what you know about me, why that would be a horse of a different color."

"I won't promise anything of the kind," Max replied firmly. He turned back to Vicki. "All right," he said. "You and the Hyaciths, accompanied by our co-operative outlaw, can start here and work south. Alec will start off in the opposite direction. I'll go and find Blair and then we'll divide the rest of the valley between us."

"Fine," Vicki said, but as soon as he had disappeared in the woods she added to Jenny, "It's silly for the three of us to stick together. I don't need a chaperon now that we've captured Mordy. Besides, somebody ought to do something about lunch."

"That's right," Jenny agreed. "With his finger on the trigger of a cocked rifle, Hy can keep this old bag of bones fishing beside the stream while I do a bit of hunting."

"That makes sense," Alec said with an approving nod. He set off in the direction of the overhanging cliff. "See you back at camp in a couple of hours. And let's hope we have something more tasty than those powdered eggs we had for breakfast."

Jenny prodded Mordy with her rifle. "Get going," she commanded. "If you weren't so skinny I'd pot you for lunch without a qualm."

"Now, my dear," Hy said, mildly scolding, "let's not develop cannibalistic tendencies until it becomes necessary."

Jenny sniffed. "So far as I'm concerned, the time has come. One more meal like the last and I'd be in the mood to cast hungry eyes at my own brother!"

Vicki laughed and watched them go back to the camp. Then she turned and walked thoughtfully down to the waterfall. No matter what project they started it always seemed to center around this spot. Hy had found his mastodon here; there was the cairn where they had trapped Mordy, and, less than half a mile away, lay the discouraged-looking sail-plane, one wing slanting upward, the other pointing to the froth and spray at the foot of the cascade.

Perhaps the jewels were here too, and the hidden exit. Suddenly Vicki remembered a story she had heard about a girl who had been hurled by rapids

into a cataract to land safely on a ledge under and behind the waterfall. Maybe there were several ledges behind this cascade, natural steps leading to the shelf!

To think was to act with Vicki. In another minute she was holding her breath as she ducked under the icy, thundering cataract. And wonder of wonders, she found herself crouching not on a ledge but at the entrance to a cave, curtained by foam and bubbles!

She blinked in the dim yellow light and then she pulled a torch out of her pocket and pressed the button. The slippery, slimy floor slanted steeply upward and nothing seemed to block its way.

"It's a tunnel," she gasped as she crawled along on her hands and knees. "If it ends where I think it does, all our troubles are over!"

After the first few yards, Vicki felt as though her rate of ascent must be as slow as her rise in the glider. It seemed to her that she slipped back a foot every time she gained five. The floor was covered with slime and the air as dank as an old cellar when flooded by a summer rain. When at last she had crawled to a point which she guessed must be near the rim of the shelf, the air began to grow colder and wetter, and then the beam from her flashlight was lost in dense fog.

Vicki hesitated, her knees shaking badly now. Should she try to grope her way through that thick mist? What if she suddenly found herself too late on

the edge of nothing? The tunnel might end abruptly at a point beyond the shelf, or far, far above it.

Then she forced her knees to be still and cautiously moved forward, an inch at a time. Now she was surrounded on all sides by the fog and her heart began to beat so rapidly that she had to stop. It was like a nightmare in which your racing feet force you nearer and nearer to the edge of a precipice.

"Stop it," she scolded herself through chattering teeth. "You're probably safely on the shelf right now and just don't know it."

As the panicky feeling ebbed away she gradually straightened and found that she could stand without bumping her head on the roof of the tunnel. She groped to the left; nothing. She groped to the right; nothing.

"I'm either in a big cave or on the shelf," she decided, and inched forward again. Then suddenly she was head and shoulders above the mist, staring up at a clear, cloudless sky. A cold, pitilessly steady wind was blowing from the direction of the mountain peak in the blue and white distance.

"It wasn't snowing after all," she thought exultantly, and at the same moment she heard the roar of an airplane. It was far south of her, and long before it was anywhere near enough for the pilot to see her, Vicki was flailing her arms as she signaled over and over again the one word she knew in the international code:

Helicopter!

CHAPTER XIII

Blair Is Missing

VICKI ALMOST CRIED WITH DISAPPOINTMENT WHEN the plane, without losing altitude, flew serenely on its way, high above where she was standing, half in and half out of the fog. The frantic waving of her red-sleeved arms as she signaled had caused the mist to swirl in thinning fingers away from her, and now she could see her feet.

"A lot of good that does you," she thought disconsolately as she slipped her numb hands into the mittens she had carried in an inside pocket of her sodden parka.

And then she realized to her horror that icicles were forming on the damp tendrils of her hair that curled around the outside of her hood. "I'd better get back into the tunnel fast," she decided. "Otherwise the soles of my boots might freeze to the snow."

She was miserably cold, exhausted and discouraged, and not at all sure that she had enough

strength left for the perilous descent down the steep, slimy tunnel.

And then something happened that made her forget her discomfort. The plane had banked and was coming back, flying now at a much lower altitude.

Almost without her own volition Vicki's arms began to flail again, signaling the word "helicopter." "It must be looking for us," she kept saying to herself. "It *must* be or it wouldn't have come back."

At that moment the pilot answered the question in her mind by wagging the big plane's wings in the "hello" of the air. Then a parachute descended from it.

"Emergency rations and medical supplies," she thought exultantly. "Now they saw my signal."

Another parachute floated down to disappear with the first one in the veil of mist. The plane winged on between the ice-capped mountain peaks, flying south.

Vicki did not dare wait out in the freezing cold any longer. She had no doubt that the pilot had sent a message in one of the parachutes saying that he would send back a rescue helicopter from the nearest airport.

She groped her way into the tunnel out of the bitter wind and was soon slithering backward down over the slimy stones. After her numb fingers thawed out she descended more slowly, and when she finally arrived at the bottom she found that her knees were only slightly scratched and bruised.

It was wonderful to feel warm again, so warm, in fact, that after she had ducked under the waterfall she splashed some of the icy water on her perspiring face. She slipped out of her hood and coat thinking:

"If the Barr family had known how this red parka was going to be used, they would never have sent it to me! Instead they would have sent me a wire forbidding me to accept the Alaska assignment."

As she started toward the camp she was surprised to see that there was nobody in the clearing. She had expected to find them all excitedly unpacking the parachutes. Then it dawned on her that the cords had probably become entangled in the branches of trees. If so, everyone would be in the woods. The quickest way to locate them would be to climb the tall blue spruce.

Vicki was halfway up the trunk when she saw to her delight that one of the parachutes had landed on a branch not far from the very one on which she had hung her hood the day before. She was just reaching out for it when she heard shouts, and looking down, saw Max and Alec running out of the woods.

"We're going to be rescued," Alec yelled to her.

"That's right," Max added. "The last plane that flew overhead must have figured out that we're down in a valley below the fog. Maybe the pilot saw the smoke from the campfire Jenny built up to roast something for lunch. Anyway, there was a note in

one of the parachutes saying that a Piasecki rescuer would take off from Anchorage as soon as possible."

Vicki released the other parachute and let it glide down to them. "Here come more powdered eggs," she cried, climbing down as fast as she could. "And here comes the girl wonder who found the hidden exit."

They stared up at her in speechless amazement. By the time she reached the ground, the Hyaciths and their prisoner were there too, all three panting with excitement.

"I wonder where Blair is?" Vicki asked. "Every one of us always looks up every time a plane passes over, so he must have seen the chutes." She said to Max, "Why isn't Blair with you? I thought you were going to look for him in the woods and make him help you find a way out of here."

Max shrugged. "I wasted half an hour trying to find him earlier, then finally decided to search alone for the exit you seem to have found."

"Oh, heavenly days," Jenny shouted. "You found it, Vic? It was you who signaled to the plane that came back and dropped the chutes?"

Before Vicki had a chance to reply they were all asking her questions at once. As she told them how she had ducked under the waterfall and climbed through the tunnel to the shelf, she was thinking with one part of her mind:

"Blair must have looked up when he heard that

plane fly over twice, and he must have seen the parachutes. Where can he be now?"

When she had finished answering all of their questions, Max said, "The helicopter should be here in less than five hours. Somebody ought to be up on the shelf to signal to the pilot. He may not like the idea of coming down through a veil of mist, and I wouldn't blame him. He might crack up on the shelf, so if you and Jenny will make a signal flag out of that overworked red parka of yours, Vic, I'll go on up there."

"I think the smart thing to do," Vicki said, "is for both you and Alec to go, and to keep on going until you reach the plateau."

"Wha-at?" Alec demanded. "Do you mean—do you think—are there enough belay points so we could make it to the top?"

"I don't know what belay points are," Vicki said, smiling. "But it looked to me as though there were enough natural steps so that the two of you together with the towrope could do it. You said you knew exactly where the furs were cached, Alec, and since you're both experienced mountain climbers, I don't see why you can't find them before the helicopter arrives."

"We're off for equipment," Max shouted, starting back toward camp at a run. "After climbing Mt. McKinley, it'll be a cinch!" Then he looked at Vicki. "Get into some dry duds right away," he ordered.

Alec, his face alight with hope, hurried after him.

"Let's don't waste time stopping for lunch," Vicki heard him say. "We can bring along some chocolate bars."

She turned to Jenny. "You don't have to keep your rifle aimed at Mordy any more," she said, grinning. "He's not going to run away. If he does, he won't be rescued—ever. After we leave, no more planes will be flying over here until spring."

The old prospector looked sheepishly at a point beyond her left ear. "I'd ruther spend the winter in a nice warm jailhouse than this here valley, and that's a fact."

Vicki tugged Jenny's arm. "Come on, we've got to hurry back to camp and sew our signal flag to a stick."

"If you don't change in something dry," said Jenny, "we'd better start sewing on your shroud."

Once they were out of earshot of the others, Vicki said, "I think Blair is on the trail of those jewels—maybe he has already found them."

Jenny nodded. "He's been off by himself most of the morning. And he must have been awfully absorbed by something not to have looked up when that plane flew over twice. If he had, he would have seen the parachutes and would now be among those present."

"I think he looked up both times the plane flew over just as we all always do," Vicki said. "And I think he saw the parachutes, too. But suppose that just about that time he had stumbled across the

rusty remains of a dog sled or something, wouldn't he keep right on looking?"

"He would," Jenny agreed. "In fact, he'd redouble his efforts, guessing when he saw the parachutes that we're going to be rescued sometime soon."

"That's what I think," Vicki said worriedly. "I'm awfully afraid that he's made up his mind to leave this valley with those jewels but isn't going to let any of us know that he found them."

Jenny snorted. "If you ask me, he isn't going to let Mr. Gravely know either."

"That's what worries me," Vicki said. "If he has already found them, there's nothing we can do about it. He'll disappear as soon as we land at Anchorage, and by the time Gravely and Company wakes up to the fact that he has absconded with the jewels, he will long ago have disposed of them to a fence."

"We can't let him get by with that," Jenny protested. "I tell you what. We'll remind Max at the last minute that he planned to have every one of us searched before we were allowed to board a rescue plane."

Vicki sighed. "I'm afraid that won't do any good, Jenny. When Max issued that order, he naturally meant everyone except Blair, who is, for all we know, the legal representative of Gravely and Company. We have absolutely no proof of our suspicions. If we tell Max how we feel about Blair, he'll simply laugh and say that we've been letting our feminine intuitions run away with us."

"I guess you're right," Jenny said bitterly. "And even if we could talk Max into searching Blair, it would prove nothing. As you just pointed out, for all anybody *knows*, Blair's intentions are honorable, and so, as his firm's representative, he has a perfect right to leave this valley with the jewels in his possession. What he does after we land in Anchorage is something else again."

"And pure speculation on our part," Vicki added. "Our only hope is that he may not yet have found the jewels. In that case I might be able to find them first."

It was Jenny's turn to sigh. "That isn't a hope, it's wishful thinking. Why, you haven't a prayer, honey, of finding those jewels in the few hours left to us."

"At least," Vicki said, "I have a pretty good idea of where to look."

"Where?" Jenny demanded. "Have you been keeping secrets from me?"

Vicki laughed. "I didn't mean to keep it a secret, Jenny. It's just that I haven't had a chance to talk with you alone since I went up in the glider." They were halfway back to camp now, and Vicki pointed across the sailplane to the pine grove on the other side of the clearing. "When I was up in the air this morning, I discovered that a strong current of air blows the length of this valley about the level of the shelf. It almost tore the Vixen II apart before I was able to get under it, but it is strong enough to give old man gravity something of a battle. Anyway, a

sled and driver hurtling off the plateau above wouldn't fall straight down—not by a long shot. The air current would carry them for a hundred feet at least before they hit quiet air and dropped. So if they went off the plateau where I think they did, they must have hit the valley floor where that patch of woods is over there."

Jenny stared up at the veil of mist which cut out their view of the mountain. "You're right," she said after a moment. "You've figured it out exactly as it must have happened."

Vicki smiled. "I couldn't have figured it out without the help of Vixen II. Being up in the air gave me a depth of perception I wasn't born with!"

"Well," Jenny said with a chuckle, "at least we're not up in the air any more about where to look." Then she sobered. "What makes you think Blair hasn't already found them? When last seen he was disappearing into that very grove of trees."

"I know," Vicki said, "but that was hours ago. If the jewels are there and he looked there first for them, he would have found them by the time the chutes came down. In that case he would have been one of the first to emerge from the woods, if only to avoid suspicion. My guess is that he didn't look in the pine grove at all. And is still looking everywhere else but."

Jenny pursed her full lips. "Um-m. He doesn't know that the shortest distance between two points

is a straight line from the precipice to the pine grove. Is that what you're driving at?"

"How could he know?" Vicki asked. "After all, he didn't go up in the glider."

They hurried on toward camp, and Vicki said, "Anyway, if Blair doesn't show up by the time we finish making the signal flag, I'm going to look for the jewels myself. That is, unless you think I ought to help with the dismantling of the tents."

"Heavens no," Jenny said. "Mordy, Hy, and I can break camp in no time at all. After we've packed our few possessions, I'll come and help you look. Might as well pass the time that way as any other."

"You don't sound very hopeful," Vicki said, half smiling.

"Frankly, I'm not," Jenny told her. "I think Blair has known all along that the pine grove is the place to look. He's been terrified from the very beginning that someone, mainly Hy and Mordy, would barge in there and stumble across the jewels. He was very much against the idea of you wandering around the valley looking for an exit until you promised to stay close to where Hy was digging down by the waterfall. Then he was all for it. That proves to me that he knew they weren't anywhere near Hy's mastodon bones. If he knew where they weren't, then he must have had a pretty good idea of where they were. It must have infuriated him to have been forced to spend all his time building a sailplane which never

even rose above the mist. Since he was released from that project, you can be sure he hasn't left one pine needle unturned."

Vicki's shoulders drooped tiredly. "I guess you're right, Jenny. He's probably back at camp now with the jewels safely tucked in his overcoat pockets. But if he isn't, there can't be any harm in my having a look, can there?"

Jenny nodded cheerfully. "Might as well ruin your fingernails grubbing through the dirt. I'll be biting mine until I hear the sound of that helicopter's motor!"

CHAPTER XIV

Treasure Hunt

THERE WAS NO SIGN OF BLAIR WHEN VICKI AND JENNY arrived at the camp. Max and Alec were too busy getting ready for the climb up to the plateau to notice his absence. After they had hurried away toward the waterfall with their equipment, Vicki drew Jenny aside.

"I'm going now," she said in a low voice so that neither Mordy nor the professor could hear. "I can't stand waiting another minute."

"No, you're not," Jenny said vehemently. "I've made up my mind. If anyone searches the pine grove while that young crook is still at large, it's going to be Jenny complete with a loaded rifle."

"Oh, Jenny," Vicki protested. "We aren't at all sure that Blair plans to steal those jewels. He may well be a perfectly nice young man who simply isn't at his best when stranded in a lost valley."

"In that case," Jenny said firmly, "you behave like

a nice young lady and let him find the jewels him-self. There's no telling what he might do if he caught you in that grove with a handful of rubies or what-ever."

"Why, he wouldn't do anything," Vicki said. "I'd simply tell him that I'm going to turn them over to Max for safekeeping. Which is perfectly true. I won't have to mention the fact that I'm not going to turn them over to anybody until after we land in Anchorage."

Jenny thought for a minute. "If he's honest, he can have no objection. But if he's planning to ab-scond with the jewels, he'll object like anything. That's why *I'm* going. He knows I'm a crack shot and wouldn't dare argue with me."

"You can't go," Vicki said. "You're the cook. Hy and Mordy are probably starving for lunch."

"Then they can starve," Jenny said. "Or nibble on the emergency rations, which amounts to the same thing."

Just then Mordy ambled up to them and, as though he had been reading their lips, drawled, "If you gals is goin' to beat that young whippersnapper to them jools, you'd better git goin'."

Jenny whirled on him in exasperation. "I suppose you're going to try to tell us you know where they are."

He grinned slyly. "Truth of the matter is that I don't *know*. No more than I did that there was a tunnel behind that there waterfall. I was jist bluffin'

when I claimed I knew how to git outta here. Joe, he got in and out by shanks' mare, but he never did let on to me jist how. I guess he never woulda yammered to me about his claim if he hadn't been pretty darn sure I couldn't git to it before his hand got well enough for him to no-tee-fy the govvyment in writin'. Figgered he had all the time in the world, Joe did, but I woulda paid him back fer what he did to me in the Klondike if it hadn't been fer you gals."

He chuckled, staring at a point behind Vicki's left ear. "But I don't hold no hard feelin's, ma'am. I jist about come to the conclusion that a nice warm bunk in the jailhouse is as good a place as any fer me to end my days. Better food than in the poorhouse, I hear, but not so much comp'ny. Now, if I was to do you folks a favor, do you think you gals might talk Max into fixin' things so that when Joe hears I'm in the pokey, he'll come and visit me reg'lar? He'll be rich, some day, Joe will, and maybe he'd even bring me some sourdough biscuits which I doubt I'll be served where I'm goin'. All Max has to do is put that claim back in the cairn and fergit about it. That ain't much to ask, is it, ma'am?"

"All right, all right," Jenny interrupted impatiently. "We'll do our best to persuade Max to keep Joe from ever knowing how you tried to double-cross him. Now, what's the favor you're going to do us?"

He winked. "I got a head start on the rest of you folks, and I didn't leave much ground uncovered, lookin' fer the cairn *and* the jools, *and* a way out, all

at the same time, you might say. If them jools is any-
wheres in this valley, they jist got to be in that pine
grove down there." He pointed in the general direction of the sailplane. "I was jist about to go in there
and have a look-see yestiddy when Vic comes runnin' up and shoutin' that she'd found the cairn."

"Oh, for pity's sake," Jenny cried. "Vicki already
figured out that the grove is the place to look."

Not in the least perturbed he said, "Wal, then, I
guess I can't ask no favors." He turned to Vicki. "But
I might as well warn you, they's likely to be pack
rats in that patch o' pines. You're so little and pretty,
I wouldn't be a-tall surprised if one of them varmints—"

"I'm not afraid of pack rats bothering her," Jenny
broke in. "It's that young whippersnapper who
hasn't been seen since morning. If you must go," she
said to Vicki, "I'll fire three shots from my rifle.
That'll bring Blair back to camp where I can keep
an eye on him while you're gone."

"Fine," Vicki said, and started off at a run. She
heard the three shots just as she reached the glider
and entered the grove. Deep down inside her she
didn't think for one minute that Blair would come
back when he heard the shots, *unless* he had found
the jewels. But she wasn't the least bit afraid of him.
According to Jenny's reasoning he must have
searched the grove long ago and was now searching
somewhere else. The fact that he had already tried
to find the jewels in the grove didn't necessarily

mean that they weren't there. He had been very upset when he darted into the woods after the glider
came down to roost. It seemed to Vicki that he had
not been in the mood to search patiently and carefully.

But once inside the grove she was appalled at the
enormity of her task. She pressed the button on her
flashlight, wondering where to begin. Suddenly she
felt like the mole in *The Wind in the Willows* when
he explored the wild woods. It seemed as though a
hundred pair of eyes were watching her, and laughing at her. The eyes belonged to rabbits, squirrels or
birds, of course, but still it wasn't a pleasant feeling.

Then she saw to her delight that no one had been
here recently grubbing through the pine needles.
They lay as thick and smooth as a carpet under the
trees. Vicki scuffed along, first in one direction, then
in another. Every time her toe hit a hard object, she
got down on her knees and raked frantically with
her fingers. But always the object turned out to be
a stone or a root. Each rock had to be brushed clean
to make sure that the moist earth was not hiding a
precious stone. Even the roots must be examined
carefully for they might have been the rusty runners
of a sled, deeply embedded in the rotted pine needles.

It was almost as discouraging as looking for the
proverbial needle in the haystack, and after scuffing
back and forth throughout the whole grove, Vicki
came to the conclusion that the jewels must be

buried more deeply than she had at first thought.

"I guess no one will find them after all," she reflected disconsolately, "except Gravely and Company. And Max had better tell his friend, Johnny, to bring along a bulldozer and a sieve."

Now the feeling that someone, or something, was watching her grew stronger. "Probably Mordy's pack rats," she told herself with a laugh, remembering the yarn he had spun the first day. The very idea of rats stealing the gold fillings from a man's teeth!

Gold! What else had the old prospector said about pack rats? "If you folks got anything shiny and bright, best put it under your sleepin' bags tonight. Why, pack rats is worse than magpies!"

So that's why the old prospector had told her to watch out for pack rats! He had been hinting in his sly way that what she should look for was a nest. Vicki realized now that long ago the jewels had probably been picked up by rodents. She remembered Ginny telling her that when some workmen were tearing down an old house in Fairview, they had found an ordinary rat's nest containing money that had been issued fifty years before.

Excitement swept away the uncanny feeling that she was being watched. If the jewels had been embedded in a rat's nest many years ago they might well still be clean and bright and so would be fairly easy to find. Thank goodness Mordy had already searched every nook and cranny in the rest of the valley! But where did rats build their nests?

A hollow log seemed like the most logical place in the grove to start with. And the third log Vicki peered into *was* hollow. It was so old that when she poked in the middle of it with her toe, it came apart, crumbling into dust at both ends. In a second, Vicki was down on her knees, clawing away the rotten wood, hoping but not daring to believe that she might be close to some of the long-lost crown jewels.

Suddenly her fingers scraped against something hard and sharp, something that glittered faintly in the beam of her flashlight. For a minute Vicki could not believe her luck. Then, with a gasp of surprise, she lifted out a massive tiara thickly encrusted with diamonds. Snagged on one of the points of the coronet was a long, heavy gold chain. Carefully she pulled it out of the debris, her hands shaking with excitement, and at the very end she found an enormous emerald pendant.

And then a voice behind her said, "So you found them."

Vicki was so startled that she jumped to her feet, dropping the pendant and her flashlight. In that moment of almost complete darkness her heart stopped beating and then started in again, racing so loudly that she was sure Jenny must be able to hear it back at camp.

If only Jenny could hear! For the voice, of course, belonged to Blair Brossard who must have been watching her from the very beginning, following her every move as he sneaked silently behind her,

walking on the thick carpet of pine needles. But why had he hidden from her? On Monday she had offered to help him find the jewels. He had no reason to believe that if she did find them she would refuse to turn them over to him.

He pressed the button on his own flashlight and directed the beam right into her face. Hoping she didn't look as frightened as she really was, Vicki blinked and cried out in the bravest voice she could muster:

"For heaven's sake, you don't have to blind me!"

He lowered his torch, and let the beam fall on the tiara and necklace. "So *you* found them," he said again.

Now Vicki knew that she and Jenny had been right all along in suspecting that this young man was dishonest. He was not glad that she had found the jewels; he was furious. The barely suppressed rage in his voice could only mean one thing: He had no intention of turning the jewels over to his employers. And Vicki had ruined his scheme. Even if she gave him the jewels now, she could not be expected to keep the finding of them a secret. Reporters would undoubtedly be waiting for the helicopter when it brought them back to the Anchorage airport. Within a few hours, Gravely and Company would know that the long-lost crown jewels had been found. Blair might try to abscond with them, but he wouldn't get far.

If his plan was to succeed, there was only one

thing for him to do. Vicki inwardly shuddered at the thought. It would be so easy for him to make it look like an accident . . .

But there was no sense in standing there, terror-stricken. And there was no sense in trying to run away. No one could run through those heavy branches. Screaming wouldn't do any good either; the camp was too far away. Her only hope was to stall for time. Jenny had promised to come and help her look for the jewels as soon as she had finished packing.

How long had Vicki been gone? How long would it take the Hyaciths and Mordy to finish preparations for their departure? Were they even now still eating lunch? Had Blair gone back to camp in answer to Jenny's three rifle shots and then unobtrusively slipped away again?

He reached down then and scooped up the necklace, gloating as the facets of the emerald danced in the light. "This little pretty," he muttered to himself, "is worth fifty grand."

Vicki clenched her hands to keep them from trembling. "I'm sure it is," she said, and to her surprise, her voice was calm and steady. "There are probably more jewels inside that hollow log. Let's look."

She reached down, but, misinterpreting her move, he roughly brushed her arm aside. "No, you don't," he snapped, grabbing up the tiara. "I'll do all the searching from now on."

"I was only trying to help," Vicki said meekly.

"You said yourself not so long ago that two heads are always better than one."

He glared at her, his lips curling with sarcasm. "Oh, don't try to play that game. You've been after these jewels ever since you heard about the Jenkins case. You didn't fool me with all that talk about trying to find a secret exit."

"But I did find a way out," Vicki told him, gaining courage as they talked. Maybe she had misjudged him; maybe it was he who had suspected *her* of being dishonest, instead of the other way around. That would explain why he was furious that she had found the jewels. "If you'd gone back to camp," she went on quickly, "Jenny would have told you that I found a tunnel behind the waterfall and climbed up to the shelf."

"So that's why that plane came back and dropped the chutes," he mumbled. "I figured the pilot must have seen the smoke from our campfire." Again he glared at her, his eyes narrowed with suspicion. "You may have found a way out, but since then you've been looking for these jewels. When I heard those three shots about an hour ago, I was searching in the woods just south of here. I came out and climbed up to the slope and saw someone duck in here. I had just about decided that the pine grove was the place to search anyway, so I wasted no time in joining you."

"But, Blair," Vicki said innocently, "why didn't you let me know that you had joined me? Work-

ing together, we would have saved a lot of time."

"Because I was tired," he stormed at her. "Dog-tired. Working on that silly glider all day, and searching for the jewels half the night."

"Oh," Vicki said, wide-eyed. "Then you've been searching at night?"

"Of course I have," he told her bitterly. "You don't think I've been able to sleep much since that old pack rat deserted camp, do you?"

Vicki couldn't help laughing at that. "It was a pack rat who found the jewels, all right," she said. "I would never have thought of looking in this hollow log if I hadn't remembered that Mordy said pack rats were as as bad as magpies."

"Luck," he growled. "Fool's luck. I figured that the dog sled must have been carried by its own momentum to a spot in the woods near the slope. But when I saw you duck in here a while ago, it suddenly dawned on me that this might be the place. I decided to let you do the preliminary searching for me, and after you'd given up, I'd finish the job."

"But I found them," Vicki said cheerfully. "And even if we don't find any more, you'll collect a fat reward when Max turns these over to your employers."

"Max?" he almost shouted. "What's he got to do with this?"

Vicki's eyebrows shot up in astonishment. Now was the time to prove whether or not this man was honest. "Surely," she said mildly, "you can have no

objection if these jewels are given to Max for safe-keeping. After all, he's the captain. And, as a matter of fact, I think you ought to share the reward with him."

"I'm not sharing anything with anybody," he snarled, and there was something so menacing in his attitude that it was all Vicki could do to keep from shrinking away from him. She had never liked his looks before, handsome as he was, but now she thought he was downright ugly. His lips were a white, taut line, and paralleling them, his brows met in a threatening frown.

"I'm not sharing anything with anybody," he said again, "with the possible exception of you."

"Me?" Vicki demanded, her voice quavering in spite of herself. "Why, me? As you said yourself it was just luck—"

"Oh, come off it," he interrupted savagely. He was down on his knees now, scrabbling through the dead wood of the old log. In another minute he held up a ring with an enormous ruby. "What'll you take to keep your mouth shut? This or the emerald?"

She stared at him, speechless. So he thought that she was a thief and a blackmailer!

"This is the lot," she heard him say, and numb as she was with amazement, his voice sounded very far away. "Tiara, necklace, and rings. Naturally, I'm keeping the tiara. Even after those diamonds are cut up for resale, they'll be worth a small fortune. What'll it be, the ruby or the emerald?"

"Oh," Vicki gasped. "Then you never had any intention of bringing these jewels back to your employers?"

He threw back his head, roaring with ugly laughter. "Of course not. They don't even know about the professor's share-the-flight ad. Last summer I came across that old Jenkins file when I was tracing the history of a ruby an Indian maharaja was interested in. It would never have occurred to me that there was a chance in a million of finding this valley if I hadn't seen the professor's ad. I'm not a detective, I'm a junior gemologist, and sick and tired of working with stones somebody else always gets. So I answered the ad, stuck the Jenkins file in my briefcase, and asked for an extended leave of absence, with two weeks' pay in lieu of the vacation due me. Figured that if I found the jewels, I'd mail in my resignation, and Gravely and Company would never know why. If I didn't have any luck, I could get my old job back." He chuckled. "They don't even know I swiped the file. It's a closed case so far as they're concerned and has been for many, many years."

"I feel almost sorry for you," Vicki cried impulsively. "They'll track you down in the end. A big firm like that won't spare any expense."

He laughed more loudly than ever. "Don't be a fool. I just told you they don't even know I swiped the file."

"But they will know soon," Vicki pointed out, forgetting that with every word she said, she was plac-

ing her life in danger. "Don't you realize that soon after we're rescued a description of this valley will be written up in all the Seattle papers? Mr. Gravely is bound to remember the Jenkins case then, and when he looks for the file, he'll also remember that you were one of the passengers on this expedition. It won't take him long to put two and two together."

"So what?" Blair demanded. "By that time I'll have disposed of the jewels to a fence. You can do anything if you have enough money. They'll *never* track me down!" Suddenly he stopped and stared at her. "Say, what is your game, anyway? Are you trying to tell me that it isn't safe for me to take any of the loot? You want all of it, huh? Well, you've got another think coming!" He took a menacing step toward her. "There are other ways of making you keep your mouth shut besides—"

And then a booming laugh came from the trees behind Blair.

"Nice work, Vicki," Jenny said as she pushed her way through the pine branches, a rifle in her hands and Mordy at her heels. "You got a complete confession from him with three witnesses." She aimed the rifle at Blair. "Pick up those baubles and stuff them in your pocket," she commanded sternly. "You can have the pleasure of carrying them back to camp."

For a moment Vicki thought he would bolt, but when Jenny tucked a plump finger around the trigger, he meekly obeyed, whining all the while.

"I haven't committed any crime," he pleaded. "I

only *said* I wasn't going to bring the jewels back to Gravely and Company. You should at least let me collect the reward. If it hadn't been for me, Gravely and Company would never have got them back."

"Oh, yes, they would," Jenny said, forcing him to walk ahead of her. "By this time tomorrow, everyone in Seattle will know about this valley."

"That's right," Mordy put in gleefully. "And then, as Vic was saying to herself a while back, they woulda flown in here with a bulldozer and a sieve."

They had been walking single file through the trees and Vicki turned around to stare at the old prospector. "How on earth did you know I said that?"

"Don't be silly, Vicki," Jenny said over one shoulder. "You didn't think that I'd let you roam around in here by yourself for long, did you? When Blair didn't show up after those shots, I sent Mordy after you, only he followed you through a path in the woods."

"It wasn't her I follered," Mordy said, chuckling. "It was *him*. A trail a blind Indian could foller!"

"And then," Jenny continued, "after I'd fed Hy and had a little something myself, I decided to join your search party. I got here just in time to hear our young gemologist try to bribe you. Naturally, I wasn't going to interrupt at that fascinating point in the proceedings. You were smart, Vicki, to lead him on and get a complete confession. If he'd had any sense he'd have known the game was up the minute

you found that tiara. If he wasn't such a pig he could have got by with collecting the reward."

"But I didn't lead him on," Vicki admitted. "I was simply stalling for time, hoping you'd arrive soon, Jenny."

"Well, it doesn't matter," Jenny said. "You deserve all the honors. How on earth did you find the jewels in such a short time?"

"We have Mordy to thank for that," Vicki said, and explained.

"Pack rats," Jenny exploded, and said to the old prospector, "If you were going somewhere where you could use money, I'd say you deserved a share of the reward. But since you're not, I'm going to see to it personally that Max fixes things so Joe Whatyoumaycallum never knows you tried to doublecross him."

"Thank you, ma'am," Mordy said. "Thank you kindly."

When they reached the clearing, Vicki suddenly felt so exhausted she knew she couldn't take another step. She sank wearily down by the glider. "I'll just have to rest a few minutes," she told Jenny. "But you don't have to wait."

"You've had a long, hard day, honey," Jenny said sympathetically. "Riding in a flimsy glider, climbing up a hidden tunnel to the shelf, and now capturing a jewel thief."

"She didn't capture me," Blair said disagreeably. "And I'm not a thief."

"Well, you tried hard, anyway," Jenny said with a grin. "And you must be tired too. So let's all sit and rest our weary feet. Once we get started, it won't take more than an hour to break camp, and we've still got lots of time."

After a long silence, Vicki said, "I hope Alec finds those furs. I think he's sinned, suffered, and repented, don't you, Jenny?"

Jenny sniffed. "It's his father who worries me. The disgrace will break his heart. I think that if that helicopter can only carry us in relays, Alec should be on the first flight. There's just a chance that the hotel cashier may not yet have deposited that check."

"Oh, it can take all of us," Vicki assured her. "The Piasecki rescuer can carry eight passengers besides two in the crew. And there'll be room for all our equipment."

She got up then and they all walked slowly back to camp. After the tents were dismantled she helped Jenny pack Max's kitchen equipment. As they worked, Vicki said, "You know, I don't think there'll be any disgrace, Jenny. I mean so far as Alec's father is concerned."

"Why not?" Jenny demanded. "For all the world knows, Alec postdated a check which he knew would bounce, and then disappeared from the face of the earth."

"But don't you see, Jenny?" Vicki said. "He didn't disappear purposely, and the world knows that now.

When our plane didn't return on schedule, the fact that we were missing must have appeared in the Seattle newspapers. Probably at first only in a small item, but it wouldn't take reporters long to check and find out that Alec is McKelvy Chapman's son. His name would then have appeared in headlines. Under the circumstances, I doubt if the bank has raised any hue and cry. Alec was simply prevented from making good a check which the bank knew perfectly well would be made good by his rich father if Alec was never rescued. As a matter of fact, I wouldn't be at all surprised if the hotel manager is still holding that check in his cashbox. He certainly wouldn't do anything which might mean unpleasant publicity for his penthouse tenants."

"Oh, my heavenly days," Jenny shouted, dropping the skillet to hug Vicki. "You're perfectly right. Hotel managers are the most discreet people in the world. And I think you're right, Vicki. I have a feeling Alec isn't going to do any more gambling; he's learned his lesson."

And then they heard the far-off roar of an engine. It was Vicki's turn to hug Jenny ecstatically. Now at last she could look up at that veil of mist and know that soon it would be broken by a huge sausage-shaped craft suspended from windmilling rotor blades.

The adventure that had started out as a picnic was coming to an end!

※※※※※※※※※※※※※※※※※※※※※※※※※※※※

CHAPTER XV

No Place Like Home

VICKI HAD ADMIRED THE HYACITHS' COZY SEATTLE apartment when she first visited it, but now it seemed like the most luxurious place in the world. After several days of roughing it in a lost valley, she had almost forgotten what it felt like to sink down into the depths of a comfortable chair.

"This is heaven," she told Jenny. "There's only one place where I'd be happier at the moment."

"I know," Jenny said, heaving her feet from the floor to the sofa. "The Barrs' Castle in Fairview, Illinois."

"It isn't really a castle," Vicki said, smiling. "But when we were living in our parachute tent it seemed like one to me."

"'Be it ever so humble,'" Jenny chanted. "'There's no place like home.'"

Vicki nodded. "For a long time back there I thought I was never going to see mine again. I

wasn't at all sure we would ever get out of that valley until Mordy said he *knew* how to get out. If he hadn't lied I might not have ducked under the waterfall."

"Oh, yes, you would have," Jenny argued. "You felt in your bones from the very beginning that there was a hidden exit, and you know it."

Vicki laughed. "But it was Mordy's cheerful attitude that gave me the feeling. He did know there was a way out, but he didn't know where it was." She paused. "I can't help hoping that he's like the Eskimos and will enjoy spending the rest of his days in jail."

"I do too," Jenny admitted. "I never trusted him, but you couldn't help liking the old fox. I'm glad you and Max put that claim back in the cairn so his pal, Joe Whatyoumaycallum, will never know his best friend tried to double-cross him."

Vicki nodded. "Max checked up on Joe, you know, and found that he had mangled his right hand in a trap shortly after he left the valley. So Max filed a formal claim with the government for him. With all the publicity our valley has been getting lately, it'll be swarming with prospectors."

"And scientists," Jenny added. "Hy is in seventh heaven about the whole thing. What with Alec's father backing him up, and the other trustees coming over to our side since your very generous donation—"

"You mean Gravely and Company's," Vicki inter-

rupted. "I wish you could have seen Mr. Gravely's face when Max and I laid those jewels on his desk. I don't think he believed a word we said when we called him from the Anchorage airport. Then when we produced concrete evidence in the form of Blair and the jewels, he went temporarily insane with joy. At first I thought he was going to give me the emerald pendant, but I finally convinced him that the only reward I wanted was a donation for Hy's expedition and a new Vixen for Max. Then he began scribbling checks and insisted that I accept this darling little bracelet as a souvenir."

"You did all right," Jenny said gaily. "And wasn't it grand that Alec found the furs and there wasn't any unpleasant publicity? When I saw his father among those waiting for us at the Anchorage airport I knew he must have flown back from Hawaii as soon as his son was reported missing, and guessed that he probably made that check good before it even left the hotel." She shook her head thoughtfully. "It's hard to believe that McKelvy Chapman has such a weakling for a son, but I do think Alec is going to mend his ways from now on. He looked awfully ashamed of himself when he was telling his father how he had lost that money gambling."

"He certainly did," Vicki agreed. "I was pretty sure his father would be waiting at Anchorage when we landed, as well as a crowd of reporters. That was what worried me all the time. I knew Alec's name would appear in headlines in the Seattle papers, and

I was afraid that eventually the story with all of our names would appear in the Chicago papers. And I was right, it did, the morning before we were rescued. Mother was almost wild with worry when I called her from Anchorage."

Jenny nodded sympathetically. "I can imagine, the poor lamb. But all's well that ends well, and even though Alec isn't very bright, we can be thankful that he got out of his scrape without any scandal."

"Blair wasn't very bright, either," Vicki added. "Why he stole the Jenkins file instead of making copies of those papers is beyond me. Sheer laziness, I suppose. But he must have known that if we discovered that valley on the first trip, a description of it would have been written up in all the papers. Then Mr. Gravely would have remembered the Jenkins case and looked for the file."

"And that," Jenny said, "is probably just why Blair stole it, and later threw it into the fire. He didn't want anyone else, and especially not Mr. Gravely, to read that letter. Since the case was closed years ago, Blair probably figured that the present head of the firm didn't know any of the details. In that case, Mr. Gravely might hear about a warm springs valley in the Alaska Range, but would have no idea that the long-lost crown jewels were there."

"But," Vicki pointed out, "Mr. Gravely *did* know that letter almost by heart. It seems to me that Blair

was stupid to think that his employer didn't know all of the details connected with a half-million-dollar loss."

"I see what you mean," Jenny said thoughtfully. "Blair never had a chance of finding those jewels and getting away with them, unless, as it turned out, we were stranded in that valley for several days. If we'd found it last Saturday and returned the same day, Mr. Gravely would have heard about it. By Monday he would have had an army in that valley going over it with bulldozers and sieves. Blair wouldn't have had a prayer." She pursed her full lips. "It just proves that dishonest people are always either stupid or lazy, or both." She struggled to her feet. "And now I must go see to my dinner. It's got to be perfect with such a distinguished chef as Professor Barr coming to dinner. A pepper pan roast of Olympia oysters. I do hope your father likes oysters, Vicki."

"He adores them," Vicki told her. "And I don't think he's ever tasted the Olympia variety. What are they like?"

"They're tiny," Jenny said. "No bigger than the end joint of your thumb. I cook hundreds of them in a spicy hot sauce and serve them straight from my heavy, cast-iron skillet. They're out of this world and so is my baked Alaska salmon which should be in the oven right now."

"I still can't believe it," Vicki said dreamily as she followed her hostess out to the kitchen. "Mother,

Dad, and Ginny, all flying to Seattle yesterday just to be sure I was safe and sound."

"Well, I can," Jenny said, yanking open the oven door. "The only reason they didn't fly to Alaska the minute they heard you were lost was that while they were trying to get transportation, word came over the radio that a helicopter was en route to our rescue."

"And a few minutes later," Vicki finished, "I was talking to them over the phone. Thank goodness they weren't left in suspense too long."

Jenny lifted the lid on her skillet, and a delicious, spicy odor pervaded the kitchen. "These oysters are just about ready to serve, honey," she said. "I think you'd better call the hotel and tell your family to hustle over here."

"Oh, my goodness," Vicki gasped. "And I'm still in uniform." She flew to the phone and then to Jenny's room to change into a gay print frock. She was running a comb through her silvery blond hair when she heard the doorbell ring.

It was Max, grinning with delight. "I've found Vixen III," he shouted the minute she opened the door. "The most beautiful craft I've ever seen, sitting right here at the Boeing plant waiting for me."

"I'm glad, Max," Vicki said, smiling. "And what will you do with Vixen I after she's been dismantled?"

"Retire her," he said promptly, "with an honorable discharge. If she were a horse, I'd visit her stall

every day with my pockets full of sugar and apples and carrots. You and she brought me luck, Vic. If it hadn't been for you I'd never have been able to afford the kind of air-ferry I'm going to pilot from now on."

"Don't forget Mordy," Vicki reminded him.

"I'll visit his stall too," Max said with a laugh. "Every chance I get."

And then the bell rang again. In another minute Vicki was hugging her slim, pretty mother, crooning ecstatically, "It's all settled, it's all settled. I'm to fly back with you."

"Good." Professor Barr lowered his face for Vicki's kiss. "Then you passed the tests all right?"

"Of course she did." Ginny gave her sister's arm an affectionate pat. "Lay-dees and gent-tel-men, behold Federal Airlines' pride and joy. The one and only assistant assistant flight superintendent who will spend the next few weeks in Chicago assisting the assistant interview—" she finished with a jealous pout—"interview girls who are lucky enough to be old enough to try and get jobs as flight stewardesses."

Vicki threw her arm around her, laughing. "Maybe during the Christmas holidays I can arrange things so you can spend a day or so in the recruiting office assisting the assistant assistant assist the assistant."

"Oh, Vicki," Ginny screamed excitedly. "Do you think you could? I mean, I *could* hand out the ap-

plication blanks and collect them after they've been filled in. I've had *lots* of experience doing that for our teacher in school during exams."

"I'll have to talk to my darling boss, Ruth Benson," Vicki replied evasively. "I still can't believe that I'm going to be working with her and so near home for six whole weeks."

She tucked her arm through her mother's and led the way into the Hyaciths' cheerful living room."

"Good evening, good evening," Professor Hyacith greeted the Barrs warmly. "And how did you enjoy sight-seeing in our fair city?"

"It is a fair city indeed," Professor Barr replied. "Practically air-conditioned with ocean breezes blowing from one direction and mountains protecting it on the other. Back home we're having a blizzard while you're enjoying what we would call mild spring weather."

Jenny came in from the kitchen then to welcome her guests with hearty handshakes. "Seattle is the only place to live," she informed them. "I tried to talk your daughter into getting a job with Boeing Aircraft and living with us forever after, but she would have none of it."

"And I," Max added ruefully, "tried to talk her into staying on the Juneau run forever after, and failed dismally."

Vicki grinned at him. "I wouldn't see much of you if I did," she said. "Bush pilots don't stay grounded very long."

"Are you a really and truly honest-to-goodness bush pilot?" Ginny asked Max in an awed voice. Then as she got a whiff of the delicious odors wafting in from the kitchen, her mood changed abruptly. "I'm starving," she wailed. "I've been on a diet for three whole days and I can't stand it another minute."

"A diet?" Jenny asked in a shocked voice. "How perfectly dreadful! You poor little lamb. What on earth is the matter with you that a doctor put you on a diet?"

Ginny giggled. "There's nothing the matter except that there's too much of me in certain spots."

Jenny snorted. "That's the most ridiculous statement I ever heard. I'm just about to put dinner on the table and then you can make up for those three days in one sitting."

"That's what I'm afraid of," Ginny mourned. "I'm like Vicki when she rode in the glider. For every pound I lose when I diet I generally gain five on the fourth day."

"Never mind," Vicki said comfortingly. "One of these days you'll get slim without even trying."

"That's what would have happened to me," Jenny boomed, "if we'd stayed in that valley much longer. What with helping Vicki trap the various dishonest members of our party, I hardly had time to hunt or cook, let alone eat."

"I'd be perfectly willing to starve under those circumstances," Ginny said enviously. "Nothing ever

happens to me. And I'll bet even when Vicki's working in Chicago and coming home week ends, something exciting will happen to her."

"Let's hope not," Betty Barr said, shaking her cap of curls. "That last adventure almost finished me."

"Me too," Vicki agreed. "I was so tired I slept for ten hours straight when we got back here."

But deep down inside her, she knew that the adventure in the Alaska Range would not be her last. At least, not if she could help it.